FAKE-OFF
with Fate

WHITNEY DINEEN

Made in the United States. August 2025

Print ISBN:
E-book ASIN:

https://whitneydineen.com/newsletter/

33 Partners Publishing

Dedicated to all the lovely authors in the Maple Falls series.

Ladies, we have been through it all in our year-plus writing together. Adding loved ones to our tribes, losing others, health scares, cross-country moves, and so much more. You are all amazing and I'm honored to be able to call you my friends.

Map of the Town

CHAPTER 1
ASHLYN

I LOVE MY JOB. *I love my job. I love my job.* Unfortunately, the repetition of my contentment mantra doesn't always work. Take now, for instance. I'm standing in Callista Crenshaw's palatial closet about to sort her shoes according to designer instead of style, which is not how I do things. Ever.

In my professional (and highly sought after) opinion, shoes are sorted by occasion, then heel height, and finally color. That is, if my client owns the necessary two hundred-plus pairs needed to make this system successful. Being that I'm a closet organizer for the rich and famous, ninety-nine percent of them do. The other one percent are hyper-vigilant hippy-types worried about leaving too large of a carbon footprint on Mother Earth. *They* hire me to hang their organic, hemp, handstitched-by-Ecuadorian-nuns baggy apparel (so it doesn't constrict their auras) on wooden hangers carved by the indigenous people of some remote jungle.

Callista, however, is a reality television star so she is not spending her days worried about anything other than her public image and possibly making my life miserable. I'm starting to think the latter has become her main motivation for getting out of bed in the morning.

"I want the Louboutin first," she tells me with her signature wide-eyed stare that makes me think she would make a great serial killer. You know, unsuspecting, but devious. "Then the Nikes, then the Chanel, and finally the Louis Vuitton."

I glance up from the pile of footwear mounded around me with what I'm sure is a look of total horror on my face. "You want the Nikes sandwiched between the Louboutin and Chanel?" *On what planet does that make sense?*

Her head bobs up and down nearly imperceptibly while her facial features remain immobile. I'm guessing the Botox shots she claims to get for migraines are keeping her from animating anything above her shoulders. God knows, I've never witnessed an actual expression cross her face.

Now that my whole protocol has hit the fan—which is seriously messing with my latent OCD tendencies—I might as well see if she wants me to put all the left shoes together before lining up the right ones across the aisle. No, I can't bring myself to go quite that far. "Anything else?" I ask.

"I want you to put a light pair in between two dark pairs so they stand out more." *There goes using a photo of this closet in my portfolio.* I'm tempted to ask her to not tell anyone I had anything to do with her project, but she's not the first crazy person I've worked for, and she won't be the last. I cite the movie producer who had me organize his extensive collection of dog collars by the number of studs they had. He wore the heavily embellished ones on his "special dates."

My phone rings before I can beat my head against the Macassar Ebony planking. It's my mother, but I'm not going to tell Callista that. Instead, I mutter, "These Kardashians are going to be the end of me."

Even though it's physiologically impossible for Callista to show any emotion, I know she's excited because she moves backwards and tries to block the doorway with her double zero frame. Except for her greatly enhanced chest, I'm pretty sure she still wears toddler sizes.

"Is it Kim?" she demands. "Kendall? Kylie?"

I answer the call and declare, "Kris, how are you?" Then I wink to my client and mouth the words, "I need to take this in private." I easily crawl under her emaciated arm and make my way through the bedroom. From there I walk into the bathroom and lock the door. Once I'm safely ensconced, I ask, "What's up?"

"Are you pretending I'm Kris Jenner again?" my mother demands disapprovingly. She isn't a fan of the kind of people who hire me. But let's face it, normal folks can generally figure out how to organize their own clothes.

"It's important my customers know they aren't the only bougie people I work for," I tell her while further enclosing myself in the toilet closet. Now there's no way Callista can over-hear anything. Even if her ear is pressed up against the outer door—which I'm sure it is.

"Your father is making me crazy," my mom growls.

"What now?" My parents have had an ongoing battle for the last two years, the likes of which have made me wonder if they might scrap their nearly thirty-five years together and go their separate ways.

"Dad and I were eating at the Glass Onion last night and he took four phone calls during our meal. *Four*." It's clear she feels this number is closer to a thousand than say, three.

Trying to diffuse her anger, I tell her, "Dad's busy."

"Your father is the mayor of the most darling town in the world. His whole job is cutting ribbons for the few new stores that open."

"There's more to being mayor of Maple Falls than that, Mom." I'm not exactly sure that's true, but there must be *something*.

"He approved a new stop light in town," she grumbles. "Now that the Ice Breakers are part of the NHL, traffic is getting worse."

"You see, there *is* more to it." *Although barely.*

"Ashlyn," my mom says in that warning tone of hers that she used to use right before grounding me. "I'm fifty-eight years old and your father has never put me first." Before I can respond, she adds, "Instead of taking early retirement like he promised, he decided to run for mayor. I'm sick of playing second fiddle to, well, everyone."

It sounds like she's getting ready to make a move. "You aren't going to leave him, are you?"

"I just might."

"Mom …" Even though I've been worried about my parents' marriage, I truly thought things would work themselves out.

"I'm fifty-eight years old," she repeats. "And I look darn good. I'm still young enough to find a partner who thinks I'm worth spending time with."

My hands suddenly feel sweaty, which is a sign that real panic is setting in. "Please give Dad another shot," I beg. "I'm going to get married and have kids some day and I don't want to have to split holidays between my in-laws *and* you and dad. You'd hardly see your grandkids that way." I know I'm playing dirty pool but so be it. Desperate times and all …

"I don't know what else to do. Your father knows how I feel, but he refuses to make any concessions. I deserve better."

"Why don't you go away together?" I ask.

"He won't leave his stupid job long enough to do that. He thinks he's indispensable, like Maple Falls would fall to ruin if he isn't on constant standby." Her sarcasm makes it clear she doesn't think that's the case.

My brain spins with viable solutions but all I can think of is, "There must be a vice mayor who can take over."

"Vice mayor? This is Maple Falls, not New York City."

"Who's next in line, then? You know, should Dad be *unable to fulfill his duties*." I giggle inwardly at the image of my dad as the hopeful first runner up in the Miss America Pageant— where I first heard that line. I used to always envision the girl in second place turning rogue and hiring someone to run over the reigning queen with a semi-truck so she could inherit the crown.

My mom interrupts my reverie. "I suppose the comptroller, but she's on maternity leave."

"And then?"

She releases a low hum like she does when she's deep in thought. "There's Gerald, but he has gout. According to his wife, he could be out for weeks." I don't even bother asking what Gerald's position is. For all I know, he might be the janitor.

In a final attempt to save my parents' coupledom, I offer, "I could come home and help." Not only am I enormously organized—as my profession would indicate—but my dad has been trying to sell me on the benefits of elected officialdom ever since he became mayor of Maple Falls. Of course, that's primarily because he thinks my job is ridiculous and nobody, no matter how wealthy, needs a closet organizer. Little does he realize the entire ecosystem of Hollywood is based on such triviality.

"You would do that for me?" The relief in my mom's voice is apparent.

"I would do anything for you," I assure her. Also, I do not want to be the thirty-two-year-old daughter of divorced parents. Especially because I know that deep down my mom and dad really do love each other.

"How fast can you get here?"

All I have left in Callista's closet are the shoes, so I tell her, "I could leave the day after tomorrow."

"You'd better come tomorrow. I'm not sure how much more of this I can take."

"I love you, Mom," I tell her. "Don't issue any ultimatums until I get there."

"We'll see."

A crisis of this order is the only thing that keeps me from trying to convince my client that her concept of orderliness is total chaos. Leaving the bathroom, I make quick work of placing three hundred and twelve pairs of shoes in such a way, one might think they were swept up by a tornado and dropped willy nilly from the sky. Okay, it's not that bad, but it's still horrendous.

At five o'clock, I walk out of my client's Beverly Hills compound and drive home to pack. All the while, I say a silent prayer my mom keeps her cool long enough for me to figure out how to save her marriage.

CHAPTER 2
JAMIE

TRYING to relax into the lumpy cushions of the ancient sofa that came with my rental, I click the link on my phone sent to me by the editor of the *Maple Falls Gazette*. It's the article about my recruitment to the Ice Breakers.

Coach Dale Hauser of Maple Falls' very own Ice Breakers has just announced his choice for captain, Jamie Hayes. Hauser tapped Hayes for this coveted position on his newly minted NHL team, claiming, "There's no one I trust more to lead my guys to victory. Jamie is a straight arrow who knows the importance of teamwork. I'm excited to be working with him again."

Hayes comes to us from the New York Blades where he played center for the last six years. Before that, he was with the Chicago Flame. He started his career at the University of Illinois in Chicago where he first played under Coach Hauser.

I recently spoke with Jamie, who told me, "I'm looking forward to getting to know all the guys and can't wait to work with Dale again. I owe my continued love of hockey to the dedication he showed to my college team. There are few role models like him left."

I continue to skim the rest of the article, hoping it will help to soothe the potential ruffled feathers of my new teammates. I understand from Dale that more than one of them was vying for the position of captain. While it's common practice that the captain is one of the players who has been with the team the longest, this team is new. As such, they need a leader who's had the most experience.

With the exception of Cade Lennox, who also played for the Blades, I haven't ever been on the same team with any of them. It will be novel to play with them instead of against them like in years past.

I've always admired Weston Smith, who was traded from the Tennessee Wolves. He's a really determined guy, which is something you need to succeed in this sport.

Then there's Carson Crane, who's one of the few hockey players I've ever heard of that's from the south, which is not at all common in our sport.

As for me, I most likely would have stayed with the Blades until retirement had my girlfriend not left me for the billionaire she met on a recent fashion shoot in Martinique. After her desertion, I seized the opportunity to get out of Dodge and nurse my wounds in a more secluded location.

There's only one problem with my new situation. I'm a city guy, through and through, and Maple Falls is tiny. Seriously, I feel like I've been kidnapped and taken to the woods to be held until my ransom is paid.

I'm renting a small cabin while I figure out what part of town I want to live in. So far, nothing compares to my apartment in New York, which is in the old meat-packing district, halfway between Chelsea Market and the Whitney Museum. Twelve-foot ceilings, with weathered brick walls and giant casement windows. Just add bamboo floors and an outdoor space and it's the perfect find. I'm leasing it out to a former teammate during the season so I can have it available in the off-season.

In Maple Falls, I have the choice of residing in the woods or living in town. As far as I've been able to discern, the two are not that dissimilar. Seriously, I have never seen this many trees.

I'm so distracted contemplating my questionable domestic situation that I practically jump when the landline rings. And here I thought the old phone was nothing more than decoration. Picking it up, I stare at it like it's going to bite me. "Hello?" I say somewhere near the vicinity of the giant mouthpiece.

"Is this Jamie Hayes?" a gruff voice inquires.

"It is."

The tone immediately becomes more jovial. "Jamie, this is Mayor Thompkins. I'd like to welcome you to Maple Falls!"

I suppress the burst of laughter bubbling up inside of me. If receiving a call from the town's mayor doesn't smack of hick living, I don't know what does. "Thank you," I tell him. "It's nice of you to take the time to reach out."

Before I can find a way to cut the call short, he says, "I'd like to invite you to join me for supper tomorrow night. You know, give you the rundown of our little paradise."

I have no idea why he thinks I need that information, although I'm guessing Dale would support my attendance, so I tell him, "That would be nice. What do you have in mind?"

"What are you in the mood for?" he counters. "We have Italian, Chinese, pizza, a sweet little diner that serves the best burgers this side of the Mississippi ..."

Before he can finish regaling me with more options, I interrupt him. "Burgers sound great."

"Meet me at Shirley May's on Main Street at seven," he says. "I can't wait to tell you all about Maple Falls." Then he hangs up.

Picking up my cellphone, I press the button with Dale's face on it. He answers immediately. "I just got off the phone with the mayor," I tell him.

My statement is met with a snort of amusement. "Bill Thompkins is nothing if not eager."

"So you've already talked to him?"

"Once, and it was a lot." *Shoot, maybe I didn't need to take this meeting.*

"It sounds like you don't want to join us," I say disappointedly. "What could he possibly want to talk to me about?"

"He doesn't want *you* to talk at all. He'll spend about two hours telling you the history of Maple Falls and then if I had to guess he'll ask you to co-chair Maple Fest."

"Maple Fest …"

"It's an annual event that put Maple Falls on the map before the Ice Breakers." He's quick to add, "It's supposedly a lot of fun, but if I were you, I wouldn't get involved."

"You don't have to worry about me." Co-chairing a small-town festival sounds like as much fun as being a grand marshal of a parade—which is something I've done and don't ever need to repeat. So. Much. Horse. Poop.

"You ready to meet some of the guys tomorrow?" Dale asks. "The whole team isn't here yet, but those who are have already started some preliminary practices. They're a great group."

Instead of answering his question, I ask one of my own. "How's Harry Franks handling my arrival?" Harry and I played college hockey together, and we didn't get on. While we were decent teammates, our personalities clashed. I'm charming, and he's more like a viper on blades.

"He's not exactly thrilled you're joining us, but he'll take it on the chin."

"Thanks, Coach, that's a real comfort."

"Seriously, Jamie, Harry's a good guy if you give him a chance. In fact, I think the two of you might just turn out to be great friends."

I'm sure he's wrong, but I don't tell him that. Instead, I say, "Harry has a hard time with boundaries."

"You mean because he asked out your college sweetheart?"

"While I was still dating her," I remind him.

Dale laughs. "If I remember correctly, she didn't go out with him."

Defending my position, I tell him, "He should have never tried to get her to."

"All's well that ends well," he drawls.

There's nothing like a trite platitude. "If you say so."

"Why don't we meet at Shirley May's in town for breakfast in the morning before we head to the arena? That way I can give you a little history on some of the guys."

"That's where I'm having supper with the mayor," I tell him.

"It's good eating for a town this size," he assures me before adding, "See you at ten in the morning. And Jamie, thanks for joining the Ice Breakers. I know it couldn't have been easy for you to leave the Big Apple, but this is going to be a great move for you. I just know it."

Instead of telling Dale how much I needed to get out of New York, I say, "I'm thirty-five. This is my last stop as a pro. Not only do I love working with you, but I like the idea of my hockey career coming full circle."

I can tell he's touched because he pauses like he's trying to suppress emotion. "Maybe once you're done playing, you'll consider being my assistant coach."

"That's a real compliment, Dale, but we'll have to wait and see. New York is still my home and it's the only place I've imagined living out my retirement."

"You never know, you might meet a nice local girl and settle down right here in Maple Falls."

"And I might grow wings and take up cliff jumping." I hurriedly add, "And you know heights aren't my thing." Getting involved in a romantic relationship is not on my to-do list. In fact, it's not on my radar at all.

Undeterred, Dale says, "I know it sounds farfetched, but word is there's something about this town that sparks love in the hearts of hockey players." He backs up this pronouncement by adding, "The first year the Ice Breakers' charity team played, every unattached player got hitched. And they met their intended right here in Maple Falls."

"There must be a lot of single gals here." I cringe inwardly at the thought. I'm not in the headspace to fight off female adoration—which unfortunately comes hand-in-hand with being a professional hockey player.

"There not always *from* here," he says. "But this is definitely where the guys are getting bitten by the love bug."

"You'd better watch out, or you might be next," I tease.

"I wouldn't mind that at all, son. In fact, I'd like to meet a nice lady to spend my downtime with."

"Good luck," I tell him. "But I'm not looking."

With a note of warning in his voice, he tells me, "That's exactly when Cupid sends his arrows flying."

I don't bother responding to such a ridiculous statement. Instead, I tell him, "I'll see you tomorrow, Dale." Then I hang up.

I may finish my hockey career in Maple Falls, but I guarantee I will not fall in love here.

CHAPTER 3
ASHLYN

AS I DRAG my luggage out of my house, my Uber driver feels the need to comment, "You sure don't travel light."

I stare down the walkway at him while cocking my go-to-war eyebrow—the left one. "I'm just taking what I need."

"Are you going away for a year?"

"Are you hoping to get a tip?" I counter. Seriously, if I had enough time, I'd send him on his way and call for another ride.

His attitude changes quickly and he hurries to put my things in the trunk before opening the back door for me. "I'll get you there in one piece *and* on time."

"Can you get me there without further conversation?" I want to know.

Instead of taking the hint, he asks, "You got a boyfriend?"

As far as I'm concerned, the only real downside of living in LA is the subpar pool of eligible men. It's not that there aren't any single guys, because there are. It's just that most of them are busy trying to date gorgeous girls in their twenties. Even the fifty-year-old, fat, bald ones think they're entitled to romance movie stars and supermodels. Cute as I am, the only ones asking me out are usually waiters hoping for their big break. I've had two of those dump me as soon as they met someone they thought could advance their careers.

For the fun of it, I lie, "I have a girlfriend." Then I embellish, "She's a three-hundred-pound body builder. I'm pretty sure she could take you." That does the trick, and I get to enjoy the forty-five-minute drive to LAX in relative peace.

The two-hour flight to Washington whizzes by and with each passing mile I feel myself decompress a little more. I haven't been back to Maple Falls in two years. My mom has visited me several times, which I suppose is why I haven't felt the need to go home sooner.

Meanwhile, my dad has stayed home to keep the town from falling to ruin in his absence. This intense devotion is the primary reason I'm worried he won't go away with my mom and choose to risk his marriage instead.

At the airport I pick up a rental car so that if my parents don't leave town as hoped, I'll have a vehicle at my disposal. This might be pessimistic thinking, but just because I want something to happen, doesn't mean it will.

Driving through the familiar countryside, I realize how much I love Washington state, especially in the fall when all the leaves start to change color. The sight of the emerging orange tint causes a feeling of pure contentment to fill me. So much so, I can almost taste all the goodies I used to devour at Maple Fest. I don't expect to be here long enough to enjoy my hometown's longstanding celebration, but I make a promise to myself to come back for it next year.

Passing Main Street feels surreal. Everything is just as quaint and homey as it was the last time I was here. Maple Falls could be on the cover of a coffee table book spotlighting the charm of American towns.

I'm looking forward to spending some time in the bookstore before hitting the diner for my favorites. More than anything, I can't wait to put my boots on and go for a walk in the woods. As much as I enjoy mountain hikes around LA, nothing compares to the forest surrounding my parents' house.

Unfortunately, my peaceful contemplation doesn't last long. As soon as I turn down the road to my childhood home, I spot my mom standing on the porch. She's throwing handfuls of clothes onto the lawn. Pulling in the driveway, I ram the gearshift into park as she yells, "I told you that if you made one more dinner engagement during the weekend I was going to leave you!"

I look around for my dad, but I don't see him. My mom rants, "But I've decided I'm not going. Instead, you are!"

Getting out of my rental, I glance around to see who she's talking to, but there's no one there. "Mom?" I approach her slowly like I'm going to attempt to disarm a robber who's hopped up on speed. She seems *that* unpredictable.

My older doppelgänger, by twenty-six years, turns around with such force, she nearly falls into the bushes. "Ashlyn, thank God you're home!" She dumps the remaining load of clothes onto the ground before running toward me with her arms open. Once I'm locked in her embrace, she announces, "You can help your dad pack. He's moving out."

Taking a step backwards, I stare at her angry expression. My mom is very pretty. The only noticeable changes to her appearance in the last decade are the slight greying of her auburn bob and the tiny crows' feet forming around her large green eyes. Other than that, she looks just like she did when I was growing up—beautiful.

"Dad is moving out?" I ask in disbelief. *So much for waiting until I got home to try to fix things.*

"He doesn't know it yet, but he sure is."

Putting my arm around her narrow shoulders, I turn her around and lead her back up the stairs and into the house. For the time being, I leave my dad's belongings strewn about the yard. "I thought you weren't going to give him an ultimatum yet. What happened?"

"He just called and told me he wouldn't be joining me at the Elliots' dinner party on Friday night because he's taking the new captain of the Ice Breakers out to eat instead."

"Why does he need to take a hockey player out?" I ask this even though I'm pretty sure I know the answer.

My mom confirms my suspicions. "Maple Fest."

Like the rest of us, my dad has always loved Maple Fest, but ever since he became mayor, he's been downright maniacal about it. "Maybe he can go out with the captain another night," I suggest.

My mom shakes her head with such force she nearly loses her balance again. "I'm done giving him chances, Ashlyn. He knew we had plans, and he went ahead and chose to do something else."

Oh, dear. "Why don't you go upstairs and take a bath?" I suggest. "Maybe take a glass of wine with you." *Or a bottle.*

Her head starts to move in a slow nod before it gains speed. "Good idea."

As she strides toward the kitchen, I yell after her, "I'll just get my stuff and unpack." But instead of going to the car, I walk out onto the porch and sit down on the swing. Pulling out my phone, I peruse last minute travel sites in search of someplace to send my parents so they can begin to repair their relationship.

On the third site, I find the perfect getaway—one week in sunny Barbados. The hotel has several small cottages on the property which are nicely isolated from the main building. I impulsively book one of them starting this weekend. That means they need to leave here tomorrow night. Luckily, I find the perfect flight, but the only seats left are in first class. Using all my air miles, I buy the tickets and pray I can pull this off.

Instead of taking my luggage up to my old childhood bedroom, I hurry to pick up my dad's things off the lawn. Then I get back into my car and point it in the direction of Maple Falls Town Hall. I don't think I can convince my mom to go away with the man who's causing her such distress, which means I'll have to start with my dad and hope for the best.

Driving through town, I notice there are actually two new traffic lights which triple the previous number we had. The town seems busier, too. More stores have popped up in the last two years, which I take to mean that Maple Falls' population is increasing.

Parking on the street in front of Town Hall, I get out and climb the steps two at a time toward the impressive three-story white cement edifice that is the governmental hub of our town. The Greek columned building lends a certain grandeur that far exceeds the norm for small-town Washington.

Once inside, I look for a sign that will take me to the mayor's office. When I don't see one, I stop a serious looking woman wearing a black pantsuit. "Can you please tell me where I'd find the mayor's office?"

Her eyes narrow slightly before she responds, "Second floor. Third door on the right after you get off the elevator."

"Thank you." I turn and walk the direction of her pointed finger. Once in the elevator, I realize I haven't been in this building since my fifth-grade class came here on a field trip. And then, instead of absorbing the wonders of local government, I spent most of that day pining over Jeremiah Hornsicle.

When the doors slide open on the second floor, I turn right and enter the door marked "Mayor's Office." Approaching the counter, I make eye contact with a stuffy-looking character. He must be about my age but that's where any similarity ends. He looks like he just walked out of central casting for the role of nerd in *High School Musical*. If the black-rimmed glasses and argyle sweater aren't bad enough, this dude is wearing white socks with black pants.

I school my features in an attempt not to show any judgment. He might be very nice and simply have a poor fashion sense. "I'm here to see the mayor."

Without glancing up from his computer screen, he asks, "Do you have an appointment?"

"I don't, but I'm his …"

Before I can say "daughter," he snaps, "Then he can't see you."

"But I'm his …"

He finally makes eye contact. "Mayor Thompkins is very busy. You'll have to call and make an appointment."

I resist the urge to fling myself over the counter and put this loser in a headlock. "I would appreciate it if you would tell Mayor Thompkins that his *daughter* is here." I emphasize my status like I'm the crowned princess of Maple Falls returning to the palace after a lengthy tour of the continent.

His eyes open wider as he looks me up and down slowly. *"You're* Ashlyn Thompkins?" As if I'm special enough for anyone to impersonate.

"I am," I tell him. "And I'd like to see my father. Unless, of course, you think he's too busy."

Instead of responding, he stands up and walks through the first door in front of him with near military precision. I hear him say, "Mayor Thompkins, I'm sorry to disturb you but a woman claiming to be your daughter is demanding to see you." *Claiming? Demanding?* Who is this troll?

Almost immediately, an older and slightly rounder version of my dad pops through the door. "Ashlyn, what are you doing here?"

I sprint around the counter to give him a big hug, before telling him, "We need to talk."

CHAPTER 4
JAMIE

I START to get antsy after hanging up with Dale. If I were still in Manhattan, I'd burn off steam by hitting the streets and running down to the tip of the island and back.

While I suppose I could stroll through the woods behind my house, I'm a little nervous I might lose my way. Also, my city-boy upbringing has me concerned I might run into a mountain lion, or God forbid, a bear. While studying up on this part of Washington, I discovered that black bears are common. And even though Google claims they're "generally vegetarians" and not "normally" dangerous to humans, I think it's safest to assume any bear will try to eat me given the opportunity.

My fear of the local wildlife is why I decide to head over to the ice arena where the team practices. I'm not looking to chat with anyone quite yet, but I'd like to get a lay of the land. Grabbing a baseball cap, I put it on and hope it will be enough of a disguise to keep me from being recognized.

The stadium is only a mile from the house I'm renting, so I'm there in record time. It would probably take me thirty minutes to drive the same distance in New York City, which is why I take the subway there. I don't drive unless I'm going upstate for a long weekend. Then it takes a minimum of two hours to go thirty miles.

Getting out of the car, I stop for a few minutes to appreciate the bucolic scenery. The whole landscape is full of the most amazing evergreens. If I'm going to live here, I'm going to have to find a proper guide to teach me the ins and outs of surviving in the woods.

Walking into the stadium, the first person I see is Troy Hart. Troy retired from the game years ago and moved to Washington. He and his wife are raising their four sons here. In addition to owning the Ice Breakers, they also own the stadium where the team practices. Forgetting my intention to stay anonymous, I walk up and greet him. "Troy, how are you, man? It's been years!"

He looks up from his phone and grins ear to ear. "Jamie! We're so excited you agreed to join us." He reaches out and pulls me in for a hug. Then he pats me on the back enthusiastically.

"I'm looking forward to the change of pace," I tell him.

"You won't regret it," Troy says. "I don't ever want to go on vacation because every day in Maple Falls feels like the perfect getaway."

"You're like a walking advertisement for happiness, aren't you?" I'm only half-teasing. There's an aura of contentment around Troy that's quite appealing. I wonder how long it will take for me to feel the same way, if that's even possible.

He shrugs his shoulders. Like he's reading my mind, he says, "Give yourself a few months and you'll know exactly what I mean."

I grimace slightly. "I'm worried I'll get bored. What do people do around here for fun?"

"There are some decent restaurants, a movie theater, and even a world-class bookstore," he brags. "Trust me, you'll get used to things pretty quickly."

"Dale says you own a lodge here, too. You going to run for mayor next?"

He rolls his eyes. "Heck, no. Bill Thompkins is the perfect man for that job."

"Dedicated and pushy?" I guess.

With a laugh, he responds, "You must have already met him." His phone rings before I can tell him about my brief conversation with the mayor. Troy looks at his screen before pressing a button to send the call to voicemail. "It's just my brother, Zach. He can wait." He rolls his eyes before adding, "He and his wife are expecting their third child and he's in a constant panic about what they'll do when the kids outnumber them."

Before I can make an uninformed comment about children, he tells me, "We have a lot of high school and college teams scheduled to come up for hockey clinics and to see the Ice Breakers play. I know they'll be excited to meet you."

"I've always enjoyed talking to kids who love the game," I tell him. Then I add, "With the Ice Breakers in town, Maple Falls must be on the precipice of some pretty big growth." At least I hope they are. I'm starting to second-guess my decision to rusticate.

Troy shakes his head. "Most of the woods around here were donated to the town when old Victor MacDonald died." He explains, "Victor was one of the first settlers of Maple Falls. When he passed and the town took ownership of the land, they protected most of it from being developed. That way our little hamlet will stay just the way we like it."

Super. "Do you have any idea where Dale is?" I ask.

"If he's still here, he's probably in the locker room." He points down the hall. "Just follow the signs."

I reach out and shake Troy's hand. "I'm happy to see you again, man."

"You'll have to join my family for supper some night soon," he says with a smile before walking off.

I've barely been in Maple Falls for a day, and I've already made plans to meet three people for meals. At this rate, I'm guessing food will be the focus of my social life. Not that I'm complaining, I love food. I just can't imagine a small town like this will have the kind of variety I'm accustomed to.

Instead of going to the locker room, I decide to head into the arena to see if any of the guys are there. That's where I discover several players are scrimmaging. Sitting on the bleachers, I kick my feet up in front of me and watch the action. Even though everyone is geared up, I still recognize a couple of faces.

"Weston, watch your left!" Lucian shouts loudly as the puck races forward. His teammate reacts stealthily and with determination. Weston lunges to block the incoming missile, and I know from experience he's probably relishing the feel of the hard rubber as it smacks against his pads.

With a sudden movement, he deftly passes the puck to another teammate. The receiver takes control, gliding gracefully across the ice. He weaves between defenders with skill you only see in the pros. My blood starts to pump in excitement at what is about to happen.

With a final flick of the wrist, the shooter sends the puck sailing right past the goalie and into the net. The winning side raises their arms in victory, and the goalie shouts out, "That's the last time, Grazer! You're not going to pull that move on me again!"

"I've heard that one before," the shooter laughs.

I like what I'm seeing. Dale is nowhere in sight, so it's clear these guys can play without a babysitter. Hopefully, that means they get along reasonably well. Which would be a major accomplishment for any pro hockey team.

Instead of heading down toward the boards to greet the guys, I stay put and watch as the dynamics continue to play out. A player I know to be Canadian shouts out, "I'm gonna tap you like a maple tree and make syrup out of you!" The two things I know our neighbors to the north love more than anything are maple syrup and poutine.

The guys separate into small groups to work on passing drills. Lucian tilts his blade down to securely cup the puck. This is a move that will ensure the biscuit stays controlled on the stick and remains primed for quick release.

Next, he shifts his weight from the back of his feet to the front before executing the pass. His follow-through is flawless, which is clear when the disc hits its intended target. In this case, the player he's passing to.

The only thing better than watching hockey is playing it, and I can't wait to get onto the ice with my new team. But for now, I simply continue to observe the different personalities I'm expected to lead.

Leaning back, I get comfortable and while away the next hour. Any sense of trepidation starts to slip away as I follow the players' progress. I'm confident I'm going to get on well with these men.

If only Harry Franks wasn't one of them.

CHAPTER 5
ASHLYN

I CAN'T HELP but fixate on my dad's excessively cluttered desk. Leaning forward, I start to tidy it up, putting the pens in one container and the paperclips in another—*why does this man have so many paperclips?*

Meanwhile, he's prattling on about this year's Maple Fest. I'm barely listening when he says something about trying to talk the single members of the Ice Breakers into sponsoring a kissing booth to bring in more people from outlying towns.

"No one does kissing booths anymore, Dad. People are too afraid of catching a cold or God forbid, getting hoof and mouth disease." Don't even get me started on Covid.

My father looks appalled. "They don't kiss with their mouths open, for Pete's sake."

"So, they pay to get a kiss on the cheek?" I want to know. What century is my dad living in?

He shakes his head. "Just a light peck on the lips. There's no, you know ..." He pauses dramatically before saying, "... tongue."

"Mouth on mouth is enough to pass along any number of unsavory illnesses," I tell him with authority. "Trust me, a kissing booth is a bad idea."

Instead of agreeing with me, he asks, "Why are you home? Did I know you were coming?"

"You didn't," I tell him. "Because I wasn't planning on being here."

His gaze narrows noticeably. "Then why *are* you here?"

After making a couple final tweaks to his desktop, I sit back and tell him, "I'm here to save your marriage."

His face contorts into an expression of shock. "What in the world are you talking about?" He clearly has no idea what he's facing when he gets home. This either means my mom has not made her feelings clear, or my dad truly isn't paying proper attention to her. I predict the answer isn't much of a conundrum.

"You and Mom had plans with the Elliots tomorrow night, and you canceled in order to take a hockey player out to dinner."

"I need the new captain's support if I'm going to get him onboard with my kissing booth idea for Maple Fest."

"No kissing booth, Dad," I remind him sternly.

He huffs loudly. "I was also going to ask him to co-chair this year's festival."

Rolling my eyes, I tell him, "You don't have to do it tomorrow night."

"Fine," he relents. "I'll go to the stupid dinner party if it will make your mother happy, but I won't like it." He continues, "Chuck Elliot will spend the whole night yammering about how he thinks the town should plant creeping thyme around all the lampposts. Who even cares about nonsense like that?"

You might think my dad would, considering he's so preoccupied with all things Maple Falls, but I don't tell him that. Instead, I inform him, "Mom doesn't want to go anymore." His look of confusion prompts me to clarify, "She's busy throwing all of your clothes out onto the front lawn."

My father stands up so abruptly his chair shoots out from beneath him and slams into the wall behind him. "What do you mean, she's throwing my stuff out? How will that look to the neighbors?"

"I'm pretty sure she doesn't care. As far as Mom's concerned, the two of you are over."

Beads of sweat start to appear on his forehead. "She's leaving me because I was going to miss one stupid dinner party?"

"She's leaving you because she doesn't feel valued by you anymore," I explain. "You take calls when you're out to eat; you make your own plans when you already have ones with her; and from what she told me last month, you don't even tell her that you love her anymore."

"I love her!" he says with heat as his face reddens. A sure sign he hasn't bothered to tell her.

"Apparently, you don't show it."

He takes several steps and retrieves his chair before rolling it back to his desk. Then he sits back down. "*This* is why you came home?"

I nod my head. "I thought the price of a plane ticket was worth trying to help you save your marriage."

"I'll reimburse you." He's clearly missing the point and I'm suddenly not so inclined to listen to his side of things.

"Dad," I tell him plainly. "If you don't take extreme measures, Mom is going to leave you. That's it."

"I said I'd go to the stupid dinner party!"

"And I told you that won't be enough."

He reaches for a tissue from the box across his desk. Wiping his brow, he asks, "What do I have to do, climb a mountain and shout my love from the highest peak?"

If his current state of fitness is any indication, he'd probably have a heart attack after the first few feet. "You have to go away with Mom and make her your sole priority. I mean it. No telephone. No television. No computer. Just Mom."

He looks so appalled I almost laugh out of sheer nervousness.

"No phone?" he demands.

"Mom doesn't feel like you see her anymore." I stare at him

intensely as though daring him to tell me I'm wrong. Luckily, he's smart enough not to.

My dad is quiet for a long moment before he finally concedes. "I'll sit down with your mother and get something on the calendar."

"That's not going to be enough. You can always cancel something that isn't set in stone."

"What do you want me to do, Ashlyn? Leave today?" It's clear he doesn't see this as an option.

"That's exactly what I want you to do."

"We won't be able to get a reservation anywhere last minute." Then a slow smile crosses his mouth. "Unless we go up to the lodge."

My father is a bigger idiot than he's been letting on. "You can't take Mom away right here in Maple Falls. Your preoccupation with this town is the problem." Before he can protest further, I tell him, "I bought you airline tickets and reserved you a bungalow in Barbados. You leave at ten o'clock tomorrow night. You can reimburse me for *those* tickets."

He jumps to his feet again. Putting his middle finger and thumb together, he makes a loud snapping sound. "Your mother can't expect me to leave town just like that!"

"She doesn't expect it because she doesn't know about it."

"Then why do I have to go anywhere?"

"Because you want to save your marriage?" I remind him. I have heartfelt sympathy for all the years my mom has had to put up with this.

Pacing back and forth in front of me, he says, "If she doesn't know about the trip, why do you think she wants to go?"

"She doesn't want to go," I assure him. "She wants to leave you."

"What about my job?"

"What *about* your job?" I demand.

"I'm needed here!" He says this like Maple Falls is on fire and he's the only person in a fifty-mile radius with a garden hose.

"Surely, you can leave for a week."

"A week! There's no one who can take over!" *Is it me, or has my dad always had this enormous sense of self-importance?*

"*I'll* take over."

His eyes widen with surprise. "You'd actually be a very good mayor."

"You've mentioned."

"If I agree to this, and that's a big if, no one can know I've left town."

I'm starting to think he might be having some serious cognitive issues. "Why can't they know you're gone?"

"I will not have the citizens of Maple Falls feel they aren't important to me." *Yet, he doesn't seem to mind if that's how his wife feels.* "If I agree to this, you have to pretend like I'm still here."

"How in the world will I do that, Dad?"

"When people call, tell them I'm in an important meeting and that I'll get back to them." He looks at the calendar on his desk. "You'll have to meet with the Ice Breakers' captain tomorrow night, too."

"I'll reschedule that one for you."

He shakes his head with intensity. "No. You have to go. Tell Jamie I'm dealing with a crisis and couldn't make it myself. Get him to agree to co-chair the festival this year."

At this point, I'm willing to do whatever my dad wants just to get him to make things right with my mom. "Fine. I'll come to work and cover for you. Now, will you convince Mom to go away with you?"

My father's complexion turns so gray, it looks like he's about to expire on the spot. "Yes. Fine. I'll do it. Just text me the details of our trip."

"I'll text them to Mom, *if* she agrees to go with you." I reach out my hand and demand, "Give me your phone."

He looks affronted. "I will do no such thing. How will I be able to call anyone?"

"You'll have Mom's phone," I remind him.

"But she won't let me use her phone unless it's an emergency." His eyes widen as the reality of my plan starts to sink in. He tries one last time. "You can't seriously take my phone."

"Hand it over," I order. Once I have ownership of his most prized possession, I point toward the door. "Let's go. You're going to need every minute you can get to convince Mom you're serious about being a better husband."

CHAPTER 6
JAMIE

ROLLING OVER IN BED, I turn off my alarm while simultaneously releasing a loud groan. It was so quiet last night I barely slept. I'm used to falling asleep to horns honking and sirens blaring, not being serenaded by crickets.

While throwing my legs over the side of the bed, I can't help but flirt with the idea of canceling my meeting so I can go back to sleep. Yet I truly am looking forward to seeing Dale, so I push myself to shower and get dressed. Then I drive to the diner.

I find a parking spot right out front. Getting out of the car, I notice this town is even more charming than I first thought. The brick buildings look like they're from the early part of the last century. Even the streetlights are vintage.

Walking into the restaurant, I discover it's as old-school as it gets. The flooring is so dinged up it's probably original to when the establishment opened, which appears to be sometime circa 1970. It's not fancy, but I still approve. People clearly aren't coming for the ambience, so the food must be solid.

A waitress, who looks to be in her mid-to-late fifties, greets me as soon as I walk in. Her greying hair is pulled back into a tight ponytail and she's smiling with a genuineness you don't usually find from service staff in New York City.

"Welcome!" she says brightly. "Just you today?" In the Big Apple this question would likely be met with an eye roll and a large dose of attitude. Like one sorry sucker sitting alone isn't worth the effort of speaking to you, let alone taking you to a table.

"I'm meeting someone," I tell her.

She grabs another menu and leads me to a prime spot in front of the window. "Can I bring you a cup of coffee while you wait? Maybe some orange juice?"

"Do you have espresso?" I ask, although I'm guessing they might not.

Her eyes sparkle like she's about to share a secret. "No, but I have hot chocolate. How does that sound?" It sounds surprisingly good, so I nod my head in approval. "You want whipped cream with that?" she asks.

I suddenly feel like I'm seven years old again. "That would be great," I tell her. As she walks away, I start to think that places like this and people like her are probably a big reason folks like living in small towns.

Dale strolls by the restaurant window which gives me a moment to observe the changes in him since we last saw each other. It's been a couple of years, but he doesn't seem any the worse for wear. He's tall and still carries himself like the commander of a naval vessel. Just by looking at him you know he's in charge of something important.

As soon as he walks through the door, he booms, "Good morning, Shirley May!" The waitress who seated me must also be the owner. "I'm meeting my captain here."

"You go on and sit down," she says. "I'll bring your coffee in just a sec."

Dale approaches the table with a smile on his face. He looks younger than his fifty-nine years. Standing up, I stretch my hand out to shake his. "It looks like small-town life is treating you well," I tell him.

He pushes my hand away and wraps his arms around me in

a hug. "It's like every day is a vacation," he says, repeating Troy's sentiment. After patting me on the back, he steps away and sits down. "How's your cabin?"

"Isolated," I tell him.

"It's a big change from what you're used to."

"No kidding. I think I heard a bear growling outside my door." I let that statement dangle in the air in hopes he'll assure me I must have been dreaming.

Instead of putting my mind at rest, he says, "Black bears. But don't worry. They'll be hibernating soon."

Even though I'm glad to have this information, I still want to know, "And until then?"

"They're filling their bellies to make it through the winter. Just don't annoy them and you should be fine."

I make a motion like I'm writing down his sage advice with an imaginary pen. "Don't annoy the bears." Then I look up at him and grunt, "I'm pretty sure I could have figured that out on my own."

"You might have, and then again, you might not have. For instance, did you know you should never play dead with a black bear? That technique only works on grizzlies."

"What do I do with black bears? Nonchalantly turn around and run for my life?"

Dale looks alarmed. "Good God, no! You never run from black bears. They may not eat you, but running ticks them right off and they could still rip you to shreds."

My appetite is decreasing with every word out of his mouth. "Should I engage them in a game of charades? Maybe ask them to dance?"

"Son," Dale says in a worried tone, "you stand big and tall and make as much noise as you can."

"And *that* won't tick them off?"

He shrugs. "It might, but it might also scare them away."

"I'm suddenly rethinking coming here."

Shirley May walks up with our drinks. It's clear she's overheard Dale because she looks at me and says, "You carry a can of bear spray with you. That way if a bear charges you, you can let him have it."

I look down at the mound of whipped cream topping my hot chocolate and smile approvingly before asking, "Do I have to wait until it charges?"

"I've lived here my whole life," she tells me. "And I've come face to face with more bears than I can count. I've never had to use the spray on them."

"You just stand tall and make noise, huh?"

She smiles slowly. "I've only done that once. The other times, I tell them that I mean no harm and that they should just move along." Even though I'm more inclined to believe her than Dale, I'm still not comfortable with the idea of making small talk with a bear. As such, I make a mental note to pick up a case of bear spray. Maybe two.

Dale interjects, "Shirley May, this is my captain, Jamie Hayes." To me, he adds, "Jamie, this is Shirley May. She's already one of my favorite people in town." I start to wonder if maybe Dale has a little crush.

Looking up, I see a slight blush cross the waitress's cheeks. "He only says that because I'm the one who brings him his food."

"And because you're downright delightful," Dale tells her. Oh yeah, he likes her for more than the burgers she brings him. "I'd like the biscuits and sausage gravy this morning," Dale tells her before handing off his menu.

Turning to me, Shirley May asks, "What about you, Jamie? You want to try the house special?"

"That sounds great. I'd also like a grapefruit juice as well, if you have it."

With a wink, she takes our menus and walks away. Focusing my attention on Dale, I announce, "Someone has a crush."

He smiles hopefully. "You think she likes me?"

I shrug my shoulders. "I have no idea. But I think *you* like *her*."

"Guilty," he says.

"So why don't you ask her out?"

"I don't want her to say no and ruin my ability to come in here and enjoy a good meal."

"Chicken," I tease.

"Wait until you try the food and then you'll understand."

I take a sip of my hot chocolate and put it back on the table before telling him, "I stopped by and watched the team practice for a bit yesterday. You weren't there."

"Oh, I was there. I was sitting across the rink from you."

I'm surprised I didn't notice him. "You wanted to check out their dynamics too, huh?"

"I figure if they don't know they're being observed, they'll make it known who I need to keep my eye on."

"You used to do that in college too," I remind him.

He nods sagely. "And it worked. That's how I figured out you and Harry Franks were a combustible combo."

"Just because I don't like the guy, Dale, doesn't mean I haven't grown up. I'm not going to stick it to him for something he did nearly twenty years ago."

"Good to hear, son. Good to hear."

We mostly make small talk for the rest of our meal, and I'm reminded what a great guy Dale is. He was a tough coach, but he was always fair and easy to talk to. I am really looking forward to playing for him again.

So long as I'm not attacked by a bear while I'm here.

CHAPTER 7
ASHLYN

MY DAD DID NOT HAVE an easy time talking my mother into going away with him. In fact, it was touch and go for a very long time. But then he got down on one knee and took her hand in his. With a level of romance and sincerity I didn't think he was capable of, he declared, "Alicia, I love you. I know I haven't been very attentive these last couple of years and I'm sorry. Will you please go away with me and let me remind you that I'm still the man you fell in love with?"

The expression on my mom's face made it clear she was torn. I wasn't sure if she was going to give in or kick him. Ultimately, she decided to give him another shot.

Even though she agreed to go on vacation, supper was still unbearable. My dad's constant chatter about Maple Fest was driving both me and my mom insane.

After supper, she stood up and announced, "You can sleep in the guest room, Bill. I'm not sharing a bed with you again until you prove you're a changed man." *Boy, is she going to be surprised when they get to Barbados and discover there's only one bed in their hut.* I didn't think it was wise to warn her.

My mom left the house this morning without telling us where she was going. It's currently mid-afternoon and she's just now getting home. I spot her unloading several bags of groceries from the trunk, so I hurry to help her. "I bought all of your favorites, Ashlyn," she says.

"Leave it to you to always be looking out for your family." That's when I notice how nice she looks. "Your hair looks great. Did you just have it done?"

She strides into the kitchen and puts the bags on the counter before waving her fingers in front of her, jazz hands fashion. "I got my nails done, too."

"Very pretty," I tell her. The fact that she's taking pains to look her best gives me hope that she's going to give my dad a real chance.

"Where's your father?" she wants to know.

"He's, um … well …" I don't want to bring up his job, but I don't see that I have a choice. "He's waiting for me at Town Hall to introduce me around."

Her expression immediately morphs into one of pure annoyance. "You tell him that if he isn't home by five o'clock that I am going to go without him. I mean it too, Ashlyn. Not five-oh-one. Five."

I nod my head and assure her, "He'll be here." And he will, even if I have to hit him over the head and drag his unconscious body home myself. But let's hope it doesn't come to that because my dad has put on enough weight that I'm not sure I'm up to the task.

Smiling at my mom, I tell her, "I better go." Then I turn around and practically sprint out the front door.

When I get to my dad's office, I'm once again met by the same man I saw yesterday. He's even less pleasant than he was before. "Miss Thompkins," he says like he's diagnosing a fatal illness.

"What's your name?" I want to know.

"Phillip. Phillip Bane. I'm the mayor's assistant." *And bane of my existence.*

My dad walks out of his inner sanctum and waves me in.

"Let's go, Ashlyn." Then he turns to Phillip. "My daughter will be helping me out this week, Phillip. Please make sure she has everything she needs."

The appalled expression on Phillip's face indicates he will do no such thing. Which is fine with me. In fact, I wouldn't mind if he got sick and took the whole week off.

"Don't worry about me, Dad. You'll be here if I need anything."

While I only said that to keep up our ruse, the words seem to panic him. "Be that as it may, I'm counting on Phillip to assist you. I have a very busy week ahead."

His assistant looks moderately confused. "You don't have a busier week than normal, sir. In fact, I'd say it looks like a light week."

"I have things scheduled that you know nothing about, Phillip," my father snaps. "Just please do as I say and help my daughter if she needs it."

Ushering me into his office, my dad shuts the door behind us before announcing, "Phillip doesn't like you."

"No kidding," I snort. "What crawled up his butt and died?"

"That's a gross expression, Ashlyn."

"In my defense, Dad, I don't like him, either."

"He's the only other person here who knows how things run, so don't annoy him." Sitting down at his desk, he pulls out a pad. "I've made a list of all my passwords. Call your mother if something doesn't work. I don't want Phillip to think you're trying to take over."

"Why not? I mean, that is why I'm here, isn't it?"

"He wants to run for mayor when my term ends. There's no telling what he'll do if he feels threatened."

"He can have the job," I assure him.

My dad smiles slyly. "I predict you're going to love pretending to be mayor so much that you'll be begging me to help *you* become the next leader of our fair town." He couldn't be more wrong, but this is not the time to set him straight.

My dad spends the next hour and a half laying out the details of his daily life, which as far as I can tell consists of nothing more than schmoozing people. So much so that he goes into every business in town twice a month and asks the store's owners how things are going. He tells me, "Even though this is my week to stay in touch, you can skip that part. You're going to have to focus all your attention on Maple Fest."

"Maple Fest is a month away. What could need to be done that isn't already in the works?"

"You'll have to contact all the vendors and confirm they're ready to roll. Then you need to make sure the generators will be delivered two days before they're needed." He keeps ticking off items until I start to think my dad does everything himself without relying on an entire committee that oversees the event.

Looking at my phone, I announce, "It's four thirty-five. Time for you to go."

"I don't have to be home until five."

"Wrong. You need to be there early to prove to Mom that you're taking this trip seriously."

My dad inhales deeply before begging, "Can't I please take my phone with me? I promise to only use it in case of emergency, and I'll never use it in front of your mother."

"You may not," I tell him plainly. "Nothing is going to happen to Maple Falls that I can't easily take care of. You, on the other hand, are going to have your hands full trying to win Mom back." I walk toward the door while making a scooting motion for him to leave. "Go. Your wife is waiting."

"Aren't you coming home with me?" he asks, like he's afraid to be alone with my mom.

I had planned to join him, but I now realize the best thing is for my mom to see my dad show up on time, all by himself. Shaking my head, I tell him, "I'm going to start familiarizing myself with your job. Get going. If you're late, you won't need me to cover for you." I glare at him meaningfully.

My dad stands up and looks at me with a hangdog expression. "Wish me luck."

"Good luck, Dad. Just remember how serious this trip is and no matter what, you are not to call me or anyone in Maple Falls. Focus all your attention on Mom. Got it?"

He inhales deeply before expelling the air like he's trying to blow out birthday candles on a cake located in the next county. "Got it."

As soon as he leaves, I sit down at his desk and look around the room. There's nothing warm or charming about this office. The furniture looks like it's standard issue from decades ago. The walls are a dirty hue of beige, and the floor is linoleum, of all things.

My first order of business will have to be sprucing the place up. Maybe I'll bring in some plants and family photos. A rug at the very least.

Before I can finish mentally redecorating, the phone rings. When it's not picked up after three rings, I reach over and do the job myself. "Mayor Thompkins' office. How may I help you?"

The voice on the other end of the line announces, "My name is Jeremy Hunt. I'm a lawyer, and I'd like to speak with Mayor Thompkins."

"May I inquire as to what this is about?"

"It's about the land Victor MacDonald left his heir when he died."

The name Victor MacDonald is legend in our town and every school-aged child hears it repeatedly during their elementary years. That's when Maple Falls history is taught. Yet, I still feel the need to confirm. "By Victor MacDonald, you mean that man who left Maple Falls all the land?"

"Mr. MacDonald did not leave Maple Falls *any* land."

"I beg to differ," I tell him. Unless Mrs. Jenson, Mr. Harper, Ms. Block, and Mrs. Carson—my first-through fourth-grade teachers—didn't know what they were talking about. And they were super confident they did.

"Victor MacDonald left his land to his heir," the voice on the other end of the line assures me.

"Which he didn't have."

"It turns out, he did," Jeremy says.

"No, he didn't. Because if he did, that person would essentially own more than half of Maple Falls."

"Correct."

My brain is starting to hurt. "Mr. Hunt. Who are you calling on behalf of?"

"Alexander MacDonald," he tells me, like I should have worked that out already. "Victor MacDonald's legal heir."

Holy heck. This sounds like more trouble than I'm capable of handling on my own. Yet if I want my parents to stay married, I have no choice but to do so. "If this is true, and of course we will have to look into it, what is it that Alexander MacDonald would like to do with the land?" I silently pray he wants to leave it to Maple Falls, but if that were the case, he wouldn't need a lawyer.

"Mr. MacDonald plans to claim the land and develop it."

Jeremy Hunt might as well have just pronounced the end of my hometown. "Mr. Hunt," I remind him, "when an heir couldn't be found after fifty years, the town took possession of the property. We've built on it. We've created preserves."

"Which is why I need to speak to the mayor."

This is where I totally and completely lose my mind. I lie, "My name is Ashlyn Thompkins. I'm the acting mayor."

"In that case, Ms. Thompkins, you should know that we are going to take legal action if Alexander MacDonald's inheritance isn't turned over to him in a timely manner."

I wonder if my mom would think this was an emergency big enough to put off her trip, but then I realize nothing short of World War III breaking out in Maple Falls would do that. And maybe not even then.

"Let me get your phone number, Mr. Hunt," I say as calmly as I can. "You can send all pertinent documents to my attention. As soon as I get them, I will consult the town council, and we will get back to you. Or perhaps it would be better if I spoke directly to Mr. MacDonald." Then I could beg him to reconsider claiming his inheritance. Not that he would but it's a solid place to start.

Jeremy Hunt sounds borderline condescending as he tells me, "Mr. MacDonald is a very busy man and doesn't bother himself with small affairs like this. He's currently overseas on business"

I'm flabbergasted anyone would consider the destruction of an entire town a small affair. Turning on my dad's computer, I do a quick search on Alexander MacDonald. That's when I discover he's a billionaire businessman who probably has a heart made from stone. I'm guessing you don't get to be mega-rich unless you put the almighty dollar above everything else—people included.

Hopefully I won't get the paperwork or hear from anyone else until my parents get home. I refuse to be responsible for something as serious as messing up the fate of my entire hometown.

CHAPTER 8
JAMIE

AFTER BREAKFAST, Dale and I head over to the arena so I can officially meet the team. He goes into his office first while I go into the locker room. That's where I run into Cade Lennox. He and I played on the same team in New York. I greet him before asking, "How do you like small-town living so far?"

Shaking my hand, he says, "I love it! It's nothing but fresh air and peace. I don't miss the big city at all."

"It's all so foreign to me," I tell him, wishing I was as excited as he is.

"I grew up in a small town, so it feels like coming home."

"I grew up in the city," I say. "I guess I'm more comfortable with cranky cab drivers and muggers." As Cade grabs his jersey and pulls it over his head, I ask, "Had any run-ins with bears?"

He shakes his head. "Not yet, but that would be kind of cool, huh?"

Now doesn't feel like the right time to share what a chicken I am, so I offer, "It sure would be something."

Once Cade finishes changing, he heads out to the ice. That's when Harry approaches me. "Jamie," he says.

I look up from my current task of pulling my socks on. "Harry."

"It's nice to see you again." He says this like he's putting a curse on me and every generation to follow.

I'm not about to fake my feelings and share his sentiment, so I simply nod my head.

"I never thought we'd play on the same team again."

"And yet here we are."

"How do you like Maple Falls?" *Why does he care?*

"It's fine," I tell him while running my fingers through my hair like I'm primping for a date.

Harry finally realizes I'm not interested in small talk because he says, "I'll catch you out on the ice." Then he walks away.

I know I'm being petty. Not only is the past long gone, but so is the girl we both liked. She and I broke up during our sophomore year when she dropped out of school and moved home to Kansas. As such, I should be able to let this grudge go. The problem is that I just don't like Harry. Not only is he cocky, but he doesn't stay in his lane. I don't respect either of those things, and the combination of the two is downright intolerable.

After leaving the locker room, I walk out to the arena. After taking off my blade covers, I glide out onto the ice toward Dale. He shouts to get everyone's attention, causing them to skate forward and form a semi-circle around him. He announces, "I'd like you all to meet your captain, Jamie Hayes."

Greetings fill the air, along with a heckle or two.

Raising my hand, I wave and tell them, "I'm really happy to be here. I know we've all come from other teams, so we're all in the same boat. But if we work together and keep our eyes on the puck, there's no reason we can't end our first season holding a Stanley Cup."

"Sounds like you've got some big plans for us." It's Harry.

"I do, Harry." Unlike him, I've been on teams that have won the most coveted prize in hockey, and it's a huge rush.

One of our defensemen, Weston Smith, cheers, "I'm all for it, man! I have actual dreams about holding the Holy Grail!"

Several other players confirm their desire to go for the gold, so I tell them, "Let's get out there and prove we can work like a well-oiled machine. I don't like show boaters, so if you don't have a guaranteed goal, pass that disc to someone with a clear line." Several heads nod in unison.

Dale interjects, "No muffins!" He references soft shots that have no power to make it to the net.

"Unless they're blueberry!" Asher Tremblay calls out.

"Chocolate chip!" Lucian Lowe votes.

In my best New York accent, I tell them, "It's bagels or nothing!"

We wind up practicing for a total of two hours, which is long enough to start building a camaraderie and see which players work best together. So far, I can't tell if there are any puck hogs, but we do have a couple of showoffs, which, of course, is par for the course in this game.

Dale calls practice, but before anyone leaves the rink, he tells them, "If any of you have concerns, please bring them to me or Jamie right away. I've never coached a brand-new team before, and I see this as a real opportunity to start the way we plan on proceeding. I want a formidable crew who know the value of communication and are willing to support one another."

He looks directly at me, before adding, "And if you have any bad blood with another player, you'd better work it out ASAP. We're grown men, not a bunch of toddlers."

Ouch. My face heats with embarrassment at that zinger. I'm not going to let Harry get to me, but even so, I realize I'm going to have to be the bigger man and make an effort to set things right between us.

Just not today.

THE BISCUITS and sausage gravy from breakfast kept me full for hours, but my stomach starts to growl as I get ready for my supper with the mayor. I'm looking forward to going back to

Shirley May's, even if it means having to listen to Bill Thompkins prattle on about his town.

After putting on my standard night-on-the-town clothes—fitted jeans, a black t-shirt, and my leather bomber jacket—I head out to my car. I don't quite make it though.

I stop short when I come face to face with a bear cub. I don't know much about bears, but I do know one thing. When you see a baby, there's a mother nearby. I consider my options as I stand on my porch. I can either put my hands up over my head and try to scare the little guy, or I can chat with him, ala Shirley May's advice. *Or*—and this route currently seems like the most appealing—I can go back inside and order a pizza. But if I do that, I'm afraid I'll never leave my cabin again.

Standing tall, I square my shoulders and start to make noise which gets the cub's attention. He stops eating the tall grass near him, then tilts his head while staring at me. I lower my voice to try to sound more authoritative, before telling him, "There's nothing to see here, little fella. I don't mean you any harm." Then I take one tentative step toward my car. When he doesn't move, I take another.

I'm halfway to my destination when I spot the cub's mother. Hand to God, my first instinct is to run for my life. But according to Dale, that's sure suicide. I inhale deeply in hopes it will bring some oxygen to my brain so I can think clearly. As I do this, the mother bear holds eye contact with me, and she moves into a standing position. Great, now she's taking Dale's advice and standing tall in hopes of scaring me. And guess what? It's working.

I'd say she's about a hundred and eighty pounds, and if she were a human, I could probably take her. But those claws of hers are giving me real cause for concern. I force myself to channel Shirley May as I tell her, "I'm going out to supper with the mayor. I don't want to be late." I take a slow step toward my car and add, "That's quite a cute baby you have there. Good job."

I swear she rolls her eyes. Then like we're gossiping over the water cooler, she opens her mouth and makes a sound like she's talking to me. I imagine she's saying, "Honey, I'd give my right paw to go out to dinner without my cub. Bring me a milkshake, would you?"

She keeps chatting while I open my car door and hurry inside. I unroll my window and tell her, "You take care now."

I hurry to lock the doors and roll up the window as a swell of relief washes over me the likes I haven't felt since I talked that guy out of jumping onto the subway tracks last year. I promised him rink-side tickets to a game if he wouldn't do it. Luckily, he was a hockey fan.

Thinking of my past close calls, I realize any of them would probably make a small-town person shake in fear. I've evaded two attempted muggings, I've been robbed at gunpoint, and I interfered in a domestic violence attack. In the last instance, I got kicked so hard by the woman I was trying to defend that I walked with a limp for a week. But now that I've come face to face with not only one bear, but two, all that looks like child's play.

I start the ignition and fool around trying to find an appropriate Spotify playlist to celebrate a successful ending to my first wildlife encounter, when my car tips violently to the side. I'm half convinced it's an earthquake, but then I glance up and see who I can only guess is the cub's father. He's huge and he does not look happy that I was getting to know his family.

I instinctively lay on the horn hoping to get the papa bear to leave me alone, but it only seems to make him madder. He slaps the side of the SUV with enough force to cause worry. Without looking in the rearview mirror, I shift into reverse and step on the gas. I'm less concerned about hitting a tree than having this beast flip me over.

Once I'm safely away from him, I put the pedal to the metal. I'm one hundred percent sure I'm not made for this kind of life and wonder if it's too late to go back to New York.

CHAPTER 9
ASHLYN

I HAVE no idea what to do about the call I just received from Alexander MacDonald's lawyer. If I talk to Phillip, he'll demand to speak with my dad—which is impossible. I can't really talk to anyone without them wanting to consult the mayor directly.

Opening my dad's desk, I pull out the list of phone numbers he left for me. The fourth name down is a woman named Marcy Fontaine. She's the town's accountant. While I'm not sure exactly how an accountant can help me, she seems far enough removed from the mayor's office that I might get some information out of her without her feeling the need to go directly to my father.

Picking up the phone on the desk, I punch in the number. It rings twice before she answers. "Marcy Fontaine Accounting, this is Marcy. How can I help you?"

"Marcy," I start slowly as I try to formulate exactly what to say to her. I finally end up with, "This is Ashlyn Thompkins, mayor Thompkins' daughter?"

"Hi, Ms. Thompkins," she says. "What can I do for you?"

"I'm helping my dad out this week and I've come across a confidential situation that I need some help understanding."

"An accounting problem?" She sounds confused and quickly

adds, "I assure you, I keep meticulous records. I can supply evidentiary documentation should you require it."

"This isn't something you did," I tell her. "But before I explain further, I'm going to need your word that you won't share any details of what I'm about to tell you."

"Of course," she says. "I'll sign a confidentiality agreement if you want."

Her offer makes it clear she's not from Maple Falls. People in small towns usually just take each other's word. Having said that, I know a lot about confidentiality agreements. I'm required to sign one before I start most of my jobs so that I'm legally bound to stay quiet about what I see in my client's homes. They don't want me to call TMZ and talk about their secret cache of whips or evening gowns. The last was the case with a governor I worked for. The dresses were his, not his wife's.

"No need to sign anything," I tell her. "But is it possible to meet for coffee somewhere outside Town Hall so we can talk in person?" *Away from snoops like Phillip Bane.*

"I don't even work at Town Hall, I'm independent," she announces. "I could meet you at Maple Grounds on Main Street in twenty minutes."

I quickly look at the clock. I have to meet the captain of the Ice Breakers across the street at Shirley May's, so it's a convenient location. "See you there."

After hanging up the phone, I quickly pull a compact out of my purse and open it before touching up my lipstick. I'm not currently dressed in business attire, so I figure the least I can do is look as presentable as possible.

I walk out of my dad's office without a backward glance. It takes fewer than two minutes to drive to my destination. After parking my car in front of the bakery, I stop to admire the decorations starting to pop up. One of the things I love about this little town is that everyone celebrates the seasons, especially autumn. There are already scarecrows appearing on the streetlamps on Main Street. In conjunction with Maple Fest, the town holds a contest for the best scarecrow. They decorate the downtown area with them until the time of judging and it's really a cool sight.

I go inside and order two hot ciders, then I sit down at a table to wait for Marcy. I forgot to ask what she looks like but even so I know who she is the minute she walks into Maple Grounds. A tallish young woman, about my age, appears. She's wearing a sleek pencil skirt and twinset. Her hair is pulled back in a no-nonsense bun. I wonder if she knows she has a pencil tucked behind her ear.

Raising my hand, I stand up and call out, "Marcy. Over here."

She turns and immediately approaches. "How did you know it was me?"

"Lucky guess," I tell her, indicating that she should sit down. Then I push over the extra cup and say, "I hope you like cider."

She smiles. "I love it. Now, what can I do for you, Ms. Thompkins?"

"I'm not sure you can do anything, but you might know who could," I tell her. "Do you know anything about the history of Maple Falls?"

She cocks an eyebrow. "I work with your dad, remember?"

After releasing a loud laugh, I announce, "So, you know everything there is to know." She nods her head. "Pretty much."

"Victor MacDonald's supposed heir has been found, and he wants to claim his inheritance," I tell her.

Marcy nearly chokes on her cider. "How can he do that? Isn't there a statute of limitations or something?"

Shrugging, I answer, "I don't know. All I know is that we need some legal advice and we need it fast."

"What does your father say?"

"My dad is ... um ... well." Based on nothing more than instinct, I decide to trust her. "My dad is out of town with my mom. I told him I'd cover for him. He doesn't want anyone to know he's gone."

"Why?"

"He says he doesn't want anyone to feel abandoned by him, but it's my guess he doesn't want to face questions regarding why he's gone away." Marcy looks puzzled, so I explain, "He's been ignoring my mom since he became mayor and he's trying to convince her not to leave him." *I hope I don't regret not asking her to sign that nondisclosure agreement.*

"This is why I like numbers so much," she announces. Before I can ask what she means, she explains, "People are complicated. Numbers aren't. Take your parents' relationship. Your father thinks he's doing the right thing for the town, but he's not there for your mother. Numbers aren't so nuanced. They just are what they are."

Marcy and I spend the next few minutes making small talk, when a familiar face walks into the bakery. It's my neighbor and old friend, Clara Johnson. We were inseparable in grade school, but we kind of drifted apart in high school. Then we went to different colleges, and we rarely saw each other after that.

"Hang on a second," I tell Marcy. I stand up and call out, "Clara!" She turns in my direction and meets me halfway. "How are you?" I ask. "It's been ages since I've seen you."

Even though she appears a bit harried, she seems happy to see me. "Ashlyn, hi. I'm okay. Actually, I'm good. How are you?"

Tipping my head from side-to-side, I answer, "Life is busy, you know?"

"Tell me about it. I have two kids, so I know something about busy." Clara got pregnant in college, which means her oldest must be around eleven now. It's strange to think of someone as young as us with a baby, let alone a middle schooler.

"My mom says you're still next door. I'm sorry about your divorce."

"Don't be sorry about Dwayne. I'm much better off without him." She rolls her eyes. "How about you? Any lucky man in your life?"

"Only Ben and Jerry and neither of them wants to settle

down," I joke. "Listen, I'm in a meeting, but I'd love to get together some night while I'm in town."

"How long are you here?" she asks. "I've been busy getting the social media set up for the new Ice Breakers team and I'm crazy busy."

"I'll be here for a week," I tell her. "But I'm right next door so just stop by some night for a glass of wine or something."

"I'll try to do that," she says. "I'm really glad to run into you, Ashlyn. Every time I look out of the kitchen window and into the backyard, I remember all the fun sleepovers we used to have out there."

"Our childhoods were charmed." I give her a quick hug and go back to Marcy who's looking at her phone.

As soon as I sit down, she tells me, "I did a little Google search. It turns out that in the state of Washington there's no statute of limitations for claiming an inheritance. If Victor MacDonald's heir is for real, he rightly owns the land that belonged to his ancestor."

My jaw unhinges for a moment and hangs open before I manage to say, "Marcy, that's half the town."

She nods her head slowly. "I know it, but I'm going to investigate whether there might not be laws governing the preservation of the town from a fiscal angle. Barring that, the only thing I can think of is trying to come up with a respectable sum of money so the town can offer to buy the land from him."

"How much does an acre of land cost around here?" I ask.

She shrugs. "It depends where the land is located. If it's in town, it'll be worth more because it can be used for businesses. If it's remote, then less." She thinks for a beat before saying, "I'd guess on average it's around five thousand dollars an acre."

My gasp is audible. "Victor MacDonald left five hundred acres. That would be two point five million dollars! How in the world would we ever be able to raise that much?"

"Even if we *could* raise it," she says, "He'd be under no obligation to accept it."

"But if we make a big enough offer," I tell her, "then he could invest in a town where he could make more money than he could ever make in Maple Falls."

"How much time do you think we have before this guy shows up in person?" Marcy wants to know.

I take a sip of my cider before answering, "His lawyer expects everything to be turned over ASAP."

"Let me see what I can find out. But you might need to make the offer before we have the actual money. Either way though, you're going to have to tell the town about this soon," Marcy says.

"You're right," I tell her. "If you can't find a solution, we're going to need the support of everyone. I can't solve this on my own."

"You can count on me, Ms. Thompkins." She leans forward and offers an exaggerated wink. I have the sense Marcy spends more time with spreadsheets than people. "I'll stop by Town Hall later to collect the necessary documents."

Looking at my phone, I realize I'm late for my next appointment, so I stand up and tell her, "Thanks for meeting me, Marcy, and good luck. I'll be in touch soon."

Then I turn and walk out of the bakery and make my way across the street to the diner. I have the captain of a hockey team waiting for me.

CHAPTER 10
JAMIE

THE MAYOR IS ten minutes late for our dinner meeting. I figure I'll give him another five and then I'll go ahead and order my food to go.

I'm about to signal to the waitress when a very pretty woman wearing jeans and an orange sweater approaches my booth. She's average height but not at all average looking. Her hair is a touch lighter than classic auburn but it's not what I'd call red. "Hi there," she says while sitting down across from me. "I'm Ashlyn."

Well, this is awkward. I wonder if she thinks I'm her blind date or something. "Jamie Hayes," I say, expecting her to realize her mistake.

"I know. You're the captain of the Ice Breakers, right?"

"I'm sorry, do I know you?"

"I doubt it, because I don't know you." She takes a sip of the water glass the waitress left for the mayor.

"If you don't know me, then why are you sitting with me?"

The question seems to startle her because she looks up and stares at me like a deer in the headlights of oncoming traffic. "I forgot you didn't know that I was meeting you instead of my father."

"You're Mayor Thompkins' daughter?" *Holy heck, is the mayor trying to set me up with his daughter? I don't care how pretty she is, that's not cool.*

"My dad got stuck in a meeting and he asked me to come in his place," she explains.

"So, you've been tasked with trying to talk me into co-chairing Maple Fest?" If I had to guess, I'd say this was intentional manipulation on the mayor's part. Little does he know I have no problem saying no to an attractive woman.

"I couldn't care less if you co-chaired Maple Fest," she says. "But if I were you, I wouldn't do it. My dad is a lunatic about that event."

Now I'm super confused. "So, you're here to tell me all about Maple Falls?"

"Nope," she says, before turning her menu over to look at it.

"Why are you here then?"

"I told you. My dad asked me to take his place," she answers. "I'm sure he'll reschedule sometime soon and try to convince you to do his bidding."

I make a move to stand up. "If we have nothing to discuss, there's no reason for me to stay."

She motions for me to sit back down. "We both need to eat. Why don't we just enjoy supper and then we can go our separate ways."

I shift nervously in my seat before telling her, "I'm not interested in dating anyone."

Ashlyn rolls her eyes. "I hear you." Then she signals the waitress. I have no idea if that means she's not interested in dating, either, or she's hoping to change my mind.

The waitress appears before I can get clarification. "Ashlyn Thompkins! When did you get home?"

"Hi, Peggy," my unexpected dinner companion says. "I got here yesterday and I'm hankering for your beer-battered fish and chips."

Peggy—yet another middle-aged waitress—writes her order

down. "You got it, honey. You want a Shirley Temple to go with that?"

Ashlyn smiles which inexplicably causes a tightening sensation in my stomach. "I can't believe you remember my favorite drink after all this time," she says.

Peggy nods her head, and with a smirk adds, "We have pumpkin praline pie on the menu tonight, as well."

Ashlyn hands her menu over. "That pie is almost enough to make me want to move home." The waitress beams at the compliment before walking away. *So much for taking my order.*

"I'd like a cheeseburger," I call after her.

Peggy stops dead in her tracks before returning to our table. Laughing, she says, "I was so excited to see Ash here that I totally forgot about you. How do you want that done?"

"Medium," I tell her. "With fries and a Sprite."

After she leaves, I turn my attention back to Ashlyn. "I don't usually get ignored. You must be something special in this town."

"No more special than every other kid who grew up here. The difference is, I didn't stay. As a result, when I come home, some of my old friends get excited."

"Where do you live?"

"Los Angeles. I went to college at UCLA, and I stayed."

"I'm from New York City."

"I go there often for work." She explains, "I'm a closet designer for rich people. A lot of my clients have homes on both coasts."

Shaking my head, I tell her, "I can't imagine needing someone to organize my closet for me."

Her gaze moves from my face to what she can see of my outfit. "Not much of a clothes horse, huh?"

It feels like she's judging me and for some reason that irritates me. "I have over fifty pairs of shoes," I brag.

"Wow." The accompanying laughter makes it clear she's not impressed.

We sit quietly for long enough that I once again think about getting my food to go. But then Ashlyn announces, "My dad wanted to talk you and your teammates into holding a kissing booth at Maple Fest to bring in a bigger crowd."

I nearly spit out the sip of water I just took. I force myself to swallow it before telling her, "That's not going to happen."

She scoffs. "I know, right?"

What does she mean by that?

She seems to realize I've taken offense because she adds, "Not that women wouldn't want to kiss you. I mean, I'm sure *some* of them would …" Just clearly not her. Which is fine, because I don't currently want to kiss anyone, *including* her.

Yet, I can't seem to help myself from boasting, "Women enjoy kissing hockey players."

"Open your mouth," she orders.

I don't know why, but I do as she instructs. She leans forward and peers inside. "It looks like you have all your teeth, so that's a plus."

"I'm still not going to volunteer my guys for a kissing booth," I tell her.

Her face crunches up like I've just offered her a worm salad. "Please don't. I've already told my dad what a disgusting idea that is."

"You don't like kissing men, huh?" *I wonder if she's gay.*

"I most certainly do enjoy kissing men," she says. "Just not strangers. And certainly not ones who've been kissing a lot of other women." She grimaces before adding, "I mean really, hockey players? Imagine where all those mouths have been."

I raise my hand in Peggy's direction. "I think I'll take my supper home." But then I remember the bear family in my yard. If I go home, I might have to eat in the car. I briefly consider checking into a hotel until they go into hibernation.

"I didn't mean to offend you," Ashlyn says.

"You don't think calling me a man whore is offensive?"

"Not you, personally," she says. "Professional sports figures in general. The single ones anyway."

"Being that I am a professional hockey player, *and* single, it seems like you're grouping me in there."

A slow smile crosses Ashlyn's face. The result is enough to cause me to nearly gasp like a heroine in a romance novel. Ashlyn Thompkins is beautiful. Her green eyes sparkle with such humor that I can't help but feel like I've been a little thin-skinned regarding her comment. Hockey players *do* have a reputation, and for a reason.

"I'm sorry," Ashlyn says. "I didn't mean to cause insult. I just don't think a kissing booth is a smart idea in today's day and age."

Peggy comes over and puts our food down in front of us. She tells Ashlyn, "I gave you extra coleslaw. I know how much you like it."

Once she leaves, Ashlyn explains, "I don't want anyone to get sick." Then she reaches across the table and picks up the discarded paper from both of our straws before crumpling it up and tucking the wad under her plate.

"Germ-a-phobe?" I ask.

"Half the world is walking around with masks on these days," she says. "I just think we're all being a bit more careful."

The cheeseburger looks amazing, and I'm suddenly ravenous. "How about we call a truce?" I ask.

"Being that I didn't know we were fighting, I'm good with that." She picks up a french fry and bites into her fish. She groans with such intensity I can't help but wonder what her response to being kissed would be like.

After taking another bite of her food and enjoying it as much as she did her first, she asks, "So, you're not married. Are you seeing anyone?"

I shake my head slowly. "No. You?"

She grunts loudly. "Not even a little bit. I don't know what dating is like in New York, but Los Angeles is a real zoo. The last guy I went out with left me for a casting director who claimed to want to hire him for a big-time soap opera."

"Did she?" I ask.

Ashlyn shakes her head. "Last I heard, he was doing soft-core porn." She snorts when she sees the look on my face. "I'm pretty sure if I ever want to get married, I'm going to have to move to Utah or something."

"According to my coach," I tell her, "Maple Falls is Cupid's headquarters, and no one is safe here."

"I suppose that's good news for the single ladies who live here, but that doesn't do me any good." With a pointed look, she adds, "People in Maple Falls don't need me to organize their closets."

"But people in Utah do?" I tease.

"Let's hope." Her smile really is beautiful. Ashlyn Thompkins has a good sense of humor, and even though we got off to a rocky start, I'm starting to like her.

"I might know of a single hockey player or two in LA, if you want me to set you up," I offer.

She fakes a full body shiver. At least I think it's fake. "I thought we'd already decided that sports figures were too free with their charms for my tastes."

"Sorry, I forgot."

"What about you?" she asks. "Are you looking?"

It seems like the whole world has been talking about Allegra and me, so I'm surprised she can't guess the answer to that question. "Do you know anything about me?"

"I know you're named Jamie and that you're the captain of the Ice Breakers." Then she takes a bite of her fish and moans again. I make a mental note to order the fish and chips next time I come in here.

"My girlfriend left me for someone else," I tell her.

She rolls her eyes dramatically. "I don't understand people who cheat. It's degrading to them as well as the person they're cheating on."

For some reason, I feel the need to share, "She left me for a billionaire she met on a fashion shoot while she was in Europe."

Ashlyn wipes her mouth delicately before announcing, "You're better off without her then." Furrowing her brow in concentration, she adds, "I might know of a couple single ladies who live in town, if you're looking."

"No, thank you."

Ashlyn's eyes suddenly pop open widely, and she announces, "Jamie, I've just had an idea!" Before I can ask what that is, she says, "I need the help of the Ice Breakers after all."

"No kissing booth," I remind her.

She shakes her head vigorously before announcing, "I have something even bigger in mind!"

CHAPTER 11
ASHLYN

I WOULD HAVE to be totally blind not to notice what a total smoke show Jamie Hayes is. Even so, I'm not interested. My whole life is in LA and as much as I claim I can't find a decent guy there, I'm not going to move for any man. If I'm meant to find love, the Universe will have to arrange for him to show up in Southern California and trip over my cart at Whole Foods.

Still, my attraction to Jamie has made me realize there's a way that he and his team *can* help Maple Falls. As the newest club to be let into the NHL, they're getting a lot of press right now. That's something we can use to help the town make the money needed to buy back our land from Alexander MacDonald.

"Jamie." I take a breath before asking, "How do you feel about bachelor auctions?"

He stares at me with those handsome big blue eyes of his, and my stomach drops like I just got off my fifth straight ride on Space Mountain. "Excuse me?"

I spend the next few minutes telling him about my phone call with Alexander MacDonald's lawyer, and the repercussions to Maple Falls if that land is claimed. Then I tell him about Marcy's idea that the town make a reasonable offer for the land so we can keep it without upsetting our entire way of life.

"You think you can raise that kind of cash by auctioning off dates with hockey players?" He teases, "You have no idea where their mouths have been."

"The Ice Breakers are all everyone is talking about these days. There must be a way we can leverage that." I excitedly add, "We could get women from all over the Pacific Northwest, or even farther, to come and bid on you. Of course, the auction will only be part of the plan." Another thought hits me. "Maybe we could have a raffle for people to win rink-side tickets. Or, wait for it …" —I pause for dramatic effect before adding—"we could host a wet t-shirt contest for the hockey players!"

"It sounds like you're going to treat us like meat."

Shaking my head, I assure him, "It's not demeaning if you're doing it for a good cause. I promise." Although what I'm really thinking is that turnabout is fair play. If anyone is going to be objectified, it's nice it won't be women. Unless they want to be, because you know, two and half mil is a lot of money to come up with.

Jamie doesn't respond right away. Instead, he takes a bite of his burger and seems to give my suggestion some serious thought. After two more bites, he announces, "I don't hate the idea. It shows we're community-minded and serious about helping our new town."

"It really does!" I tell him, eager to have him onboard.

"I'll have to talk to Dale about it first. I can't guarantee participation from the team, but I will certainly encourage them."

"Who knows?" I say. "Maybe some fabulous woman will bid on you and you'll fall madly in love. Then you can show your ex you're not sitting around pining for her."

"I'm not going to be involved," he says, like he didn't just agree that it was a good idea.

"How can you ask your teammates to do it and not participate yourself?" I want to know.

"I'm not doing it," he repeats.

Peggy's arrival momentarily breaks the tension. "You ready for your pumpkin pie, honey?" she asks me.

"Yes, please. But bring two." I glance at Jamie and tell him, "I don't share pie."

After Peggy walks away, I add, "I suppose it doesn't matter if you do it or not. I just need enough members of your team on board so that we get a lot of good press."

"When are you thinking of having it?" he asks.

"Tomorrow, if we could. But we're going to need time to get the word out. Maybe in a month?" I suggest. "I'll need to discuss it with my dad first." But not until he comes home and is on good terms with my mom.

We eat the rest of our meal with minimal conversation. I suppose we're both lost in thought. I'm thinking that as much as I hated the kissing booth idea, I'm in love with a bachelor auction. Not only are we guaranteed to make decent money, but I figure both Maple Falls and the Ice Breakers will benefit from the buzz.

When our pie arrives, Jamie declares, "One piece is big enough to feed a family of four."

"You haven't tried it yet," I tell him. Picking up my fork, I take my first bite. The creaminess of the pumpkin hits right before the powerful spice blend kicks in. Then there's the mildly salty crunch of the praline. I have never consumed anything that comes close to being as amazing as this pie.

Jamie follows suit and jabs his fork into his piece. He takes four bites before coming up for air. "They could mass produce this and make a fortune!"

"Don't you dare tell anyone that," I warn. "It wouldn't be as good if it was mass produced."

Changing the subject, he asks, "Do you live near the woods?"

"Everyone in Maple Falls lives near woods," I tell him. "But yes, my parents' house backs up against a preserve." A preserve the town apparently no longer owns. "Are you staying in the woods?" I ask.

Is it me or does the color drain from his face. "There's a bear family on the property."

"Bears roam a lot," I assure him. "Just because you see them doesn't mean they live there. Unless of course you rent from John Brady. His cabin is notorious for bear activity."

Jamie looks like he's about to cry. "My landlord is John Brady."

I can't help the bark of laughter that escapes my mouth. "Bears won't hurt you," I tell him.

"How do you know?"

I shrug. "I don't really, but it's been years since I've heard about a mauling in Maple Falls."

He gulps loudly. "Which means we must be due for another."

For a big, strong hockey player, he sure is skittish over the local wildlife. "Jamie, you'll be fine," I assure him.

He shakes his head. "I ran into an entire family of them on my way here. The male stood on his hind legs and roared at me. He almost knocked my car over."

Suppressing another giggle, I tell him, "Bears don't roar."

"He made a loud and menacing noise that sounded like a roar to me."

"He was just protecting his family," I tell him. "It's a natural reaction."

"I wasn't threatening any of them. I was just trying to get to my car without meeting an untimely end."

What a drama queen. "Black bears don't eat humans."

"According to Google, they sometimes eat meat," he says.

"Rarely, and then usually only in the spring after they've been hibernating. When they wake up starving they sometimes go a little nuts."

His eyes open widely. "Note to self: Find a permanent home away from the woods before spring."

"You'd have to rent an apartment on Main Street if you wanted to avoid the woods altogether."

"I'm not fussy."

I laugh again, which I seem to do a lot around this man. "The only people who have ever had trouble with the bears are ones who antagonize them. Just don't throw any rocks at them or approach their babies, and you'll be fine."

Jamie doesn't respond right away; he just keeps eating his pie. When he's done, he puts his fork down and asks, "What if I help them get ready for winter and leave food out for them? They'd like me then, right?"

"They'd like you so much they'd tell their friends. And then if they wanted more food and it wasn't there, they'd break into your house to get it." The poor guy looks like he's about to faint.

"Okay, I won't feed them. But you're sure they'll hibernate soon."

"Every October," I tell him. "Like clockwork."

His head bobs up and down slowly before asking, "What do you do in Maple Falls for fun?"

"You move to LA," I joke before saying, "Life is slower paced here but you can go to the movies or go out to eat. You could even join a bowling league." He doesn't look impressed, so I ask, "What do you do in New York?"

"Go to clubs, concerts, museums. The more accurate question is what can't you do in New York?"

"Do you have a Maple Festival?" I ask.

"No, but we have farmers' markets and flea markets. There are street vendors all over the city. You can even ride horses in Central Park."

I take a final sip of water before teasing, "Why in the world did you leave that kind of nirvana for Washington state?"

"I was being followed around by reporters asking me about Allegra. When Dale called and asked if I wanted to captain the Ice Breakers, I jumped at the chance to have some solitude."

"Then enjoy the solitude and quit complaining," I tell him.

"Yeah, but you know, the bears …"

"Do you need me to drive to your house with you after supper and make sure you get inside okay?" I ask.

He looks like I just offered him a winning lottery ticket. "Would you?"

Peggy drops the check before I can answer. Jamie makes a move to grab it at the same time I do. "What are you doing?" I ask him.

"Paying the check."

"Why?"

He shrugs. "I don't know, because I always pay when I go out to dinner with a lady."

I take my credit card out of my wallet and drop it on the table. "This wasn't a date, Jamie."

"I know."

"Good, so let the town pay." I'm going to keep all my receipts and let my dad reimburse me. Then I ask, "Are you serious about wanting me to follow you home?"

"Serious as a heart attack," he confirms.

After paying the bill, we walk out of the diner together. I point across the street and tell him, "I'm parked over there."

He points to a black SUV right in front of me. "I'm right here. I'll wait for you."

As I cross Main Street, I can't help but think that if I lived in Maple Falls, I might just be interested in Jamie Hayes. But since I don't, I vow to keep him in the friend zone. After all, a girl can't have too many friends.

CHAPTER 12
JAMIE

WATCHING Ashlyn cross the street to her car, I once again realize how pretty she is. It's not just her looks though. She's smart, and funny, and she enjoys her food. I firmly believe you can't trust a woman who doesn't allow herself enough sustenance. That alone should have tipped me off about Allegra. She barely touched lettuce, and then only if it didn't have any dressing on it. Yuck.

Once Ashlyn gets into her car, I bang a U-turn on Main Street and lead the way out of town toward the bear-infested property I'm renting. Normally, I'd be reluctant to let a woman know what a scaredy cat I am, but dude, these are bears.

Winding around the curves in the road, I'm captivated by the changing colors of the maple trees. While the pine trees stay green, there are enough others to promise a spectacular fall display.

I turn on my signal well in advance, so Ashlyn has warning. When I reach the mailbox at the end of the drive, I veer right and slowly make my way up the winding path. My eyes are trained in the direction of the woods, searching for unwelcome visitors.

As soon as I get to my parking spot, I turn off the ignition. I wait for Ashlyn to park next to me before opening my door. But somehow I still can't seem to force myself out of my relative safety.

Meanwhile, Ashlyn gets out of her car and stands in the path. "Are you coming?" She sounds annoyed, like she's waiting for an errant child.

I step out with an abundance of trepidation, all the while looking around for signs of trouble. Luckily, we appear to be alone. "If you just get me to the door, I'll be fine," I tell her. Ashlyn tries to hide her amusement, but she's not successful. "I realize how unmanly I must appear," I say.

"Just a little," she responds. "But I get it. This is unfamiliar territory. Once you get used to it though, you'll be fine."

"If you say so."

As soon as we reach the porch, I unlock the door. I'm about to say goodnight to her when I hear a loud rustling sound coming from the side of the house. That's when I spot the papa bear. He's standing on his hind legs again, and he's definitely looking for trouble.

Without thought, I let out the most ridiculously shrill scream. The bear takes a step back which gives me the courage to move. I open the door and push Ashlyn inside. Then I slam it shut before turning to see if she's okay. If her laughter is anything to go on, she's just fine.

"That scream ..." she starts hiccupping in what I can only assume is vast amusement at my expense.

"In my defense," I tell her, "Dale told me to make a loud noise to scare bears away."

Tears start to stream down her face. "It's just ... you know ..." She doubles over like the sheer act of standing is too much for her.

Putting my hands on my hips, I declare, "I'm aware that didn't sound very masculine." She shakes her head from side to side, so I add, "I sounded like a little girl."

She starts to answer but instead releases more laughter. She finally manages, "Not one little girl. More like … more like …" I wait patiently for the coming insult. "Twelve!"

I spread my arms wide to create the biggest space I can. "It was huge!"

"It probably wasn't any taller than you are," she says, her face still contorted by hilarity.

"It was a bear, Ashlyn," I tell her. "If it was a mugger holding a gun, I would have karate chopped the weapon out of his hand before putting him in a choke hold. Then I would have tied him up with his own shoelaces and escorted him to the nearest police station." *Take that, doubter of my manhood.* She's sniffling like she's trying to hold back a fresh wave of tears, which is really starting to tick me off.

"Is that right?" she asks in a manner best described as *mocking.*

"I'm a six-foot three, two hundred pound, highly toned professional athlete," I tell her. "So yes, that's right."

"Would you like me to show you how to deal with bears?" she asks.

"Not if you have to go outside, no." As much as I'm ticked off at her, I don't want to see her get torn to shreds.

"I'm not going to stay here," she tells me, as though my plan all along was to lure her to my den.

"Well, not forever certainly, but at least until danger passes."

Ashlyn reaches for the doorknob. On instinct, I hurry to stop her but end up placing my hand over hers. I immediately regret doing that. Her skin is so soft it's like touching silk. "Please don't go, yet. I don't want you to get hurt."

"You don't have to worry, Jamie," she tells me. "I grew up here. I know what I'm doing."

And then to my absolute horror, she walks out onto the deck. I should go with her, but I don't. Instead, I keep the door open a crack, all the while hiding behind it and praying she doesn't get hurt.

Ashlyn looks to the left where the bear is still standing. She immediately turns away and tells me, "Do not make direct eye contact for an extended period. They will take that as a challenge." Even though I've heard this from multiple sources, it's a bit difficult not to want to discern a bear's intentions in real time.

Walking down the stairs toward her car, Ashlyn calls out, "Always move away from the bear. They're more afraid of you than you are of them." She suddenly stops in her tracks and starts convulsing with laughter. Again.

"I know what you're thinking," I tell her. "You're thinking that I'm definitely more afraid than he is." She nods her head up and down to confirm my suspicions.

She finally starts moving again, and once she gets to her car, she turns back to me. "You see how easy that was?"

I point to my right. "There's the baby. Do you still feel safe?"

"So long as I don't go over to it," she says, "I'm fine." Then she teases, "But I really want to pick him up."

"Ashlyn …"

"I'm not an idiot, Jamie. Just remember walk away from the bear, don't run, don't make eye contact …"

"And don't pick up its cub."

Touching the side of her nose, she says, "Ding, ding, ding, we've got a winner!"

With her cell phone in hand, she asks, "What's your number? I'll be in touch tomorrow after you've had a chance to talk to your coach."

I give her my number before suggesting, "You might want to reach out to Troy Hart, too. He and his wife own the team."

"I don't really know them, but I suppose I can make a call."

"You must have already left when he moved here."

She smiles before telling me, "When I was a kid the arena was nowhere near the size it is now. Maple Falls is currently a thriving metropolis, compared to the town I grew up in."

"I can't even imagine such a thing. I mean seriously, this

place is tiny," I tell her as I screw up my courage and step out of the cabin. Glancing to my left, I notice the father bear is eating some leaves and seemingly minding his own business. Thank goodness.

"Says the big man from the big city," she teases. "Give it a chance, Jamie."

Standing a little bit taller, I tell her, "Oh, I'm giving it a chance I'm just having some culture shock is all."

She appears to be contemplating something carefully before she says, "Why don't you stop by Town Hall tomorrow after practice? I'll take you on a quick walking tour of Maple Falls and give you some background info." She's quick to add, "This would not be a date. This is just the mayor's daughter helping her father by performing her civic duty to make sure all the town's citizens are happy."

Having spent a few hours already getting to know Ashlyn, I wouldn't mind if it was a date. She's so different from the other women I've previously gone out with, that I start to wonder why I've never dated someone like her. I guess the answer is that professional sports players tend to be surrounded by sycophants instead of self-assured women who know their own minds. At least that's been my experience.

"That would be nice," I tell her. "I'm sure I'll be able to share Dale's thoughts about the bachelor auction by then."

She starts her car before waving out the window. "See you tomorrow."

As soon as she pulls away, I turn around to walk back into my cabin. That's when I notice the father bear standing on his legs and staring at me. Knowing that I'm inches away from safety gives me courage. "I'm not interested in causing any trouble," I tell him firmly. "I'll stay in my lane, if you stay in yours, okay?"

I know Ashlyn said that bears don't roar, but this guy apparently didn't get the memo. He releases a growl so menacing and loud that I sprint inside. Talk about feeling emasculated. It's no wonder Ashlyn assured me that getting together tomorrow wasn't a date. She's got to think I'm the biggest coward of all time.

CHAPTER 13
ASHLYN

I WOULD BE HARD PRESSED to say what kind of man I'm attracted to as I don't really have a type. Yet, there are some basic characteristics I appreciate—honesty, courtesy, hard-working, etc. Yet as far as physicality goes, I've dated tall guys, not-so-tall guys, ones who are super fit, and others who would not be described as athletic. There have been blond-haired, brown-haired and even one redhead. But as far as I know, none of them have been afraid of bears. Having said that, ever since leaving Maple Falls, I've not exactly resided in bear territory.

Driving to my parents' house after leaving Jamie's, I can't help but think about what a surprisingly nice evening we had. If I were in the market to date someone who lives in Maple Falls, he might just be at the top of my list. And as funny as it is, instead of repelling me, his bear phobia makes him seem vulnerable and human. It's cute.

I remind myself I'm not looking to settle back at home, which means I'll just have to enjoy Jamie's friendship. Hopefully, I'll be able to help him with his adjustment process, too. I had a difficult transition when I left for college. Going from a town where the highway has two lanes—one in either direction—to a city where it's common to have upwards of five lanes or more going each way, takes some adapting to.

Pulling into my parents' driveway, I spot Clara getting out of her car. She's carrying two large bags of groceries.

She and I really did have a nice friendship, and I would like to reconnect with her again. I call out, "Hey, Clara! Can you come over later?"

She startles like she didn't see me. "Sorry, Ash, the kids both have plans tonight, so I'll be playing chauffeur." She shifts the bags for a better grip. "Soon, though, okay?"

"It's got to be tough raising them alone," I tell her. In addition to being divorced, Clara's parents died when she was in college. They were in a horrible car accident that left a huge impact on Maple Falls. Obviously, it made a much greater one on their daughter.

Clara shrugs. "It's life, right? I mean, we all have some kind of trouble." Even though that's true, she has a much bigger load to carry than I do.

"Mine is not finding a decent guy," I volunteer. "At the rate I'm going, I'm not sure I'll ever be a mother." I'm not feeling sorry for myself so much as I'm trying to be relatable. Clara must think I have it made not having the kind of responsibilities she has.

"It has to be tough living in LA," she says. "You know, the land where the number of inflated egos is only rivaled by the amount of people hoping to become celebrities."

I laugh. "You got that right." I wave to her and say, "I'll catch you soon, okay?"

The reality of Clara's observation leaves me wondering what I'm doing still living in Los Angeles. But the truth is, I like it there. I like the weather, the palm trees, and having access to both the mountains and the beach. There's a lot of diversity, and a lot to do. Also, the plain truth is that I love organizing things and there are enough people in LA with enough money to keep me employed until I'm old and gray.

It's weird walking into my parents' house knowing they're gone. Going into the kitchen I open the refrigerator and pull out a bottle of wine. After pouring myself a glass, I head back out to the front porch so I can sit on the swing and enjoy it.

That's when it occurs to me that I haven't checked my dad's cell phone since I took it from him. If I'm going to pretend he's still in town, I'd better return some messages.

There are twelve, which makes me nervous that I'm going to have a hard time keeping up this ruse. I start with the most recent. It's from that goblin, Phillip. I really do not want to have any contact with that guy.

PHILLIP

Sir, I'm a little bit concerned that your daughter seems to have taken up residence in your office. She stayed long after you left, and I'm not sure that's a good idea.

I laugh when I start to type and see that my dad has programmed his title into his phone instead of just his name.

MAYOR THOMPKINS

Please don't concern yourself, Phillip. As I told you, Ashlyn will be in town for a week to help me out. She has my full consent to use my office as she sees fit.

Phillip responds immediately.

PHILLIP

But sir, why do you need your daughter? You have me.

MAYOR THOMPKINS

I don't like it when you question me. Now, if we can please be done with this, I would like to get off the phone so I can take my wife to supper.

PHILLIP

Yes, sir.

I know this won't be the last time I have to deal with my dad's assistant, but I'm hoping I can find something for him to do so that he stays out of my way. That's when I get a brilliant idea.

MAYOR THOMPKINS

I need you to go to the fairgrounds tomorrow and make a new map of the vendors' locations.

PHILLIP

We already have a map, sir.

MAYOR THOMPKINS

I want a visual map, with photographs of where everyone will be located.

The three dot ellipses comes and goes, making it clear Phillip is having a hard time coming up with a reply. After a full two minutes he finally responds.

PHILLIP

Why?

MAYOR THOMPKINS

Because that's what I need you to do.

I have no idea what my dad's relationship is with his assistant and while I don't want to do anything to harm it, I also don't need this twerp in my hair.

PHILLIP

Yes, sir.

The next text is from Mary-Ellen McCluskey. Not only is she my parents' neighbor, who lives directly across the street, she's Maple Falls' chief purveyor of information.

MARY-ELLEN

Bill, I don't want to alarm you, but Alicia was
throwing things all over your front yard
yesterday. I didn't contact you right away
because Ashlyn came out and picked
everything up. What is Ashlyn doing home?
What was your wife doing? Please let me know
if there's anything I can do to help.

There's no way our gossipy neighbor wants to help. More
like she wants the dish so she can spread it around town.

MAYOR THOMPKINS

Thank you so much for your concern, Mary-
Ellen, but there's nothing to worry about. Ashlyn
is helping me out at the office this week, and
Alicia was getting some things together for a
yard sale. Have no fear, all is well!

I spend the next thirty minutes answering the rest of the texts
from assorted townspeople. I don't give them any direct answers
to their concerns, but I try to let them know they've been heard.

I had no idea how much my dad has on his plate. If I'm going
to succeed here, I'm going to have to treat Maple Falls like it's
one big closet in need of organization.

After finishing up, I'm tempted to text my mom at the airport
to see how she and my dad are doing, but I don't want to interrupt them. I'm hopeful that without my dad having possession
of his phone, they might be busy chatting.

Before putting both of our phones away for the night, I do a
brief check on world events. I scroll through any number of
stories that make me want to take the first space shuttle out of
here, when I come upon one headline that captures my full
attention.

**Hurricane Bartholomew Barrels Down on the Caribbean:
Expected to Make Landfall Late Next Week**

Shoot, maybe I should call my parents and warn them. Yet, it's not a guarantee that the hurricane will hit Barbados. It might go north or south or even fizzle out before it reaches the land.

I decide that's not my decision to make, so I call my mom. When she doesn't answer, I look up her flight info on the airline's website and discover it departed ten minutes ago. I guess there's nothing I can do now. They're sure to find out about the coming storm when they land. If they want, they can try to change their tickets and head home. Although, truthfully, I hope they stay and patch things up.

After all, people live through hurricanes all the time. Surely, my parents can ride out one of them.

Looking up, I realize I'm no longer alone. What in the world is Marcy doing here?

CHAPTER 14
JAMIE

I SLEPT a little bit better last night. I only got up twice to make sure the windows and doors were locked. Now that Ashlyn planted that seed about bears breaking in, every time I turn around, I expect to find them eating porridge at the table.

After showering and grabbing a quick breakfast, I manage to get out of the house and down the drive without one bear sighting. I take that to mean today is going to go well.

As I pull into the arena parking lot, I wave to several guys. One of the things I like most about being on a team is the camaraderie. Hockey players get a bad rap for being hot heads, but my experience has been mostly positive. Except for Harry.

Speak of the devil. As I pull into the parking spot with my nameplate on it, I see my old nemesis getting out of his car. It's not like I can avoid the guy now that we're on the same team, so there's no use hanging back until he's gone.

Stepping out of my rental, I greet him. "Harry."

He looks startled that I'm even speaking to him. "Jamie."

We walk side-by-side into the building in total silence, which is just as awkward as you might expect. As we approach the locker room, I turn to him and declare, "In the best interest of the team, I've decided to forgive you."

"For what?" he demands.

How stupid can this guy be? "For trying to poach my college girlfriend," I remind him.

"What are you talking about, Jamie? You stole Paige from me." He can't be serious.

"How do you figure that? I started dating Paige the month after we started our freshman year." I tell him, "We met at a party in our dorm."

"Dude," Harry says. "Paige and I had our first date the week after we moved into the dorms."

I rack my brain to see if that could even be possible, but I can't come up with any reason why it couldn't. "How did you meet?" I demand.

"We took the elevator down to the cafeteria together. She ordered a biscuit, two pieces of bacon, and grapefruit." That *was* her standard breakfast.

Paige and I lived on different floors, but I do know that she and Harry were on the same floor. "Where did you go on your first date?"

"To the roof of the medical school building." There's a glint in his eye that makes me want to punch him. That's where all the underclassmen used to go to make out.

"Did you just hook up, or did you actually date?" I want to know.

"We dated." Holding up one finger at a time, he enumerates, "We went to the zoo; we went into the city to see a movie; and we walked for miles by Lake Michigan one Saturday."

A weird barrage of emotions washes over me. The main one being dread that I might have been the interloper. "Were you exclusive?" I want to know.

"Obviously not, because when you asked her out, she went." So, they weren't boyfriend and girlfriend. That's something.

"Did you date her after I started seeing her?" I ask like this might somehow lessen my culpability.

He shakes his head. "She was suddenly unavailable to take my calls."

I've spent years being mad at Harry and there was no reason to. In fact, he had good reason to be mad at me. "I'm really sorry, Harry," I tell him. "I didn't know."

He turns the tables on me and with heat, demands, "How could you *not* have known? We were together all the time."

Shrugging my shoulders, I tell him, "I don't know. I mean, I was eighteen. I was into me and wasn't paying attention to everything else going on around me."

"Clearly." Yet he must believe me because he says, "I suppose it doesn't really matter. It's all water under the bridge."

After a moment of silence, I confess, "It's going to be weird not hating you."

"Tell me about it," he agrees.

On the surface, we seem to have made peace, but I know it's going to take some time for us both to forget our past feelings. Walking in through the locker room door, I tell him, "I'll catch you later, okay?"

He nods his head once before crossing the corridor to his locker. I hurry to open mine and get changed for practice. Then I head into the office to talk to Dale. He's on the phone but he motions me to sit and wait.

Once he hangs up, he asks, "How's my captain doing this fine morning?"

Ignoring his question, I tell him, "I had an interesting supper last night."

"With the mayor?" He looks perplexed like such a thing isn't possible. "Did he tell you all about the history of Maple Falls and their love of otters?"

I wasn't quite sure how the Ice Breakers came upon their mascot but now I know it has something to do with the town's history. Shaking my head, I tell him, "The mayor didn't come. His daughter did."

"Who's his daughter?"

I spend the next few minutes telling him about Ashlyn and the news that the town is facing tremendous upheaval.

He looks nothing short of panicked. "If any part of the arena or surrounding area isn't owned by who we think it is, we could be in real trouble. We might even need to find a new stadium."

I hadn't thought of that. "I suppose that's true, but Ashlyn has an idea to try to raise enough money to buy the land back for the town." Dale's interest is clearly piqued, so I tell him about the bachelor auction.

"All the single guys should do it," he declares excitedly. "Heck, I'd do it too if there was any chance some woman would buy a date with a rough-looking fifty-something-year-old coach."

"Please," I joke. "I bet you could raise at least a hundred dollars." Dale rolls his eyes, while I ask, "Are you giving me the go ahead to confirm our participation?"

"Heck, yes!" he says. "The last thing we need is to have to move all the guys now that the season is almost here."

We head out onto the ice together. Before practice starts, Dale calls everyone over. Once they gather around, he tells them, "Guys, we're in a bit of a jam." He relays the gist of my dinner conversation with Ashlyn and tells them about the plan for us to host a bachelor auction to raise money for Maple Falls.

"Wouldn't it be easier if we just donated?" Lucian calls out. "I want to help, but I don't want to spend an evening with a strange woman if I don't have to," he jokes. "There have been enough of those, if you know what I mean." Laughter surrounds him.

"You can certainly donate, as well," I tell him. "But the idea is to utilize the press we've been getting to promote this thing far beyond local channels. If we can do that, we might just get some big money coming to town. Remember, this cause is near and dear to all of us now."

"Come on, fellas," Dale encourages. "We've all moved to

Maple Falls to make our homes here, now we're needed to help our new community. Let's do this with gusto."

A slow but sure chant starts to build. "Maple Falls! Maple Falls! Maple Falls!"

With everyone on board, I call out, "Let's hit the ice and get this practice started. Not only do we have a town to save, but we have a cup to win!"

Winning the Stanley Cup is a long way off for us, and probably not even possible given that we aren't a longstanding team who know each other's strengths and weaknesses. Yet the way to win anything is to go in with the mindset that you can't lose.

Dale divides us into two teams. I play center which means by default, I make a lot of goals. I'm also something of a wonderkid when it comes to faceoffs, or as my past team called them, Jamie's fake-offs. I have a flashy maneuver I like to use where I let the other team get the puck, then I drop back and, with lightning speed, I steal it right back. Of course, I mix it up and go for my share of discs, so my opponents never know what to expect. It's a bit of a cocky display, but it also shows my talent.

Just my luck, Harry is playing center for the other side. We come face to face in the middle of the arena with Dale acting as ref. Harry stares me down intently and asks, "Fake-off or face-off, Jamie?"

I smile back. "That's for me to know and you to find out."

As the puck drops, I skate backward, letting Harry take first possession. As soon as he tries to pass me, I dip low to the right to throw him off, and then almost immediately change my course. Reaching out with my stick, I snatch the puck right out from under him.

I don't expect him to anticipate this move, but he does. In the end, Harry steals the puck right back and sends it to one of his defensemen, who in turn glides it down the rink and slams it home.

Skating up to me, Harry says, "I guess you didn't see that one coming, huh?

Shaking my head, I tell him, "I did not."

I can't tell if he's joking, but he pats me on the shoulder and says, "Yeah, it's never fun to be on the receiving end of one of those."

I suddenly wonder if maybe Harry isn't quite ready to let go of the past like he claims.

CHAPTER 15
ASHLYN

I WAS surprised when my dad told me his office was open on Saturdays, but at least it's only a half-day. I go in early so I can be safely ensconced in the mayor's domain before Phillip shows up. That way we don't have to make small talk, or any talk, if I'm lucky.

Even though I leave the house a full thirty minutes before Town Hall opens, my plan is for naught. As I pull into the parking lot and head toward my dad's designated spot, Phillip is standing there waving me down. I unroll the window in time to hear him say, "That's the mayor's parking place. You can't park there."

Oh brother, what a busybody. "My dad is coming in late," I tell him. "I'll move before he gets here."

He steps directly into the slip so he's blocking my path. "Your father is never late," he tells me with authority, like he spends every free minute spying on my dad. Which come to think of it, he probably does. Phillip doesn't strike me as the kind of guy with an active personal life.

"That may be," I tell him. "But now I'm here to help." I glare at him with every ounce of irritation currently coursing through me. Which is a lot.

He counters. "*I* help him. That's *my* job."

"I'm sure it is," I tell him as I start to inch my rental car in his direction. He looks nervous that I'm going to hit him, but even so, he holds his own. "You want to play chicken with me, Phillip?" I ask. I'm about two feet away from tapping him.

"You wouldn't hit me," his voice quakes with uncertainty.

"You want to place a wager on that?" *Less than a foot away now ...*

He suddenly realizes I'm not faking it, and he jumps to his left before I kiss him with my bumper. "I'm going to tell your father!" he shouts.

As he turns to walk into the building, I call after him, "You're going to have to wait until he comes in."

He stops dead in his tracks and pulls out his phone like he's going to call right now. I hurry to reach into my purse to silence my dad's ring tone, but I must grab my phone instead. As soon as Phillip hits send, my dad's phone starts to blare out the weird otter song he programmed into it. I hurry to close my window in hopes Phillip didn't hear it but I'm pretty sure he did.

I turn off my dad's phone before getting out of the car. Then with my head high, I step out of my rental and walk right by dad's assistant. "Why do you have your dad's phone?" he demands.

"I don't have his phone. I have mine."

"That was the mayor's ringtone."

"How do you know it's not my ringtone, too?"

He steps closer to me. "Hand me your purse."

"I will do no such thing, Phillip." I hold my bag tightly on the off chance he tries to rip it away from me. I wouldn't put it past the little toad.

"I'm going to talk to your father about this," he declares menacingly.

"Enjoy your chat," I tell him, knowing full well he won't be speaking to my dad any time soon.

Once I'm in the building, I take the stairs up to the mayor's office, so I don't have to ride in the elevator with Phillip. After reaching my destination, I close the door and lock it. Then I call Marcy.

She answers after only one ring. "Marcy Fontaine Accounting, this is Marcy. How can I help?"

"Marcy, it's Ashlyn. Have you managed to come up with anything else regarding Victor MacDonald's land, other than the ninety-day reprieve?" I have to admit I was surprised to see Marcy on my doorstep last night, but she was way too excited about having found a small clause in an obscure law that could at least buy us a few months' time. It was a good start, but we need more than that.

"I called a lawyer, Ms. Thompkins," she tells me. "I asked about the statute of limitations rules in Washington regarding property. He verified what we already suspected. If Alexander MacDonald can prove he's Victor's heir, then the property is his. The lawyer confirmed that we have ninety days to make this happen before Alexander can go to court to make it official."

I lean back in the chair and rub my eyes in exasperation. "I was hoping there might be a loophole," I tell her while sitting down behind my dad's desk. Reaching into my purse, I pull out a couple of framed photos of my mom that I brought in with me. If nothing else, she'll think my dad wants pictures of her around. That is, if things go well in Barbados and she ever comes into his office again.

"I had a thought," she tells me. "And it's not a good one."

The last thing I want to hear is more bad news, but I suppose it's better to be forewarned, so I ask, "What's that?"

"If this Alexander MacDonald character did his research, and I'm sure he did, he'll know the Ice Breakers are now based in Maple Falls. As such, he might not take a reasonable offer. In fact, he might not take any offer."

She's right. Alexander might want to profit from the crowds that will be coming in to town. While most people will probably stay at hotels in Spokane, which is the closest city, he might use some of that land to build additional lodging and gas stations, and heaven knows what else. "I think I'd better call his lawyer and get a feel for how willing Mr. MacDonald might be to sell the land back to Maple Falls," I tell her.

"You'd better get a town council meeting on the books, too," she suggests. "You're going to have to let everyone know what's going on."

"My dad will be back in a week," I tell her. "I'll schedule it for then."

"Ashlyn." It's the first time she's called me by my first name, and it makes me nervous. "Make it for as soon as possible. We're going to need all hands on deck, right away." After a beat, she adds, "You might also want to call your father and fill him in."

"There's no way I can do that," I tell her. "He'd take the first flight out of the Caribbean and that would be the end of my parents' marriage."

"We might be facing the end of Maple Falls," she says plainly.

Kicking my feet up onto the desk, I tell her, "I pick my parents' future over the town's." I know how mercenary that sounds, so I hurry to add, "But I think with the two of us working together, we can keep things afloat until my parents get back. I mean, it's only a week away."

"Let's hope." She doesn't sound very certain and quite honestly, I don't blame her. Who in a million years would have guessed something like this would happen within hours of my dad leaving town? Or ever, for that matter.

As soon as I get off the phone with Marcy, I call the last person in the world I want to talk to. Phillip answers after the second ring. "What?"

"My dad would like you to set up a town council meeting."

"For when?"

"Tomorrow, if you can."

"Tomorrow is Sunday. What is this regarding?" he snarls.

Lying through my teeth, I tell him, "I have no idea."

"I can't just call an emergency meeting without giving people a reason." I can just imagine the pinched look of superiority on his face as he says this.

"Tell them the future of Maple Falls is at stake."

"What do you mean by that?" he spits.

"You'll have to ask my dad."

"I'll do that." Then he immediately hangs up.

I have no idea how I'm going to get through this week without committing bodily harm on that man. I've never been a violent person, and I've certainly never threatened to run somebody over with my car, but Phillip brings out the worst in me. I'm going to have to keep my distance or risk winding up in jail.

Looking at the clock, I realize I had better go home and bring my dad's car back so that people don't start to wonder what's happened to him. It could get kind of complicated playing musical cars, but Phillip has made it clear he's looking for my dad's vehicle, so I'm going to have to let him see it.

I walk right by the aforementioned bane of my existence, but I keep my eyes in front of me. I don't say a word to him. Once I get into my car, I check my dad's phone and discover the troll has texted him three times since we got to the office.

PHILLIP

Sir, are you unwell? You're never late.

Mayor Thompkins, your daughter parked in your space even though I told her that wasn't allowed.

What time can I expect to see you today, sir? I have some concerns.

The worst part of taking over for my dad is not going to be trying to save Maple Falls—it's going to be dealing with Phillip. Typing furiously, I tell him:

MAYOR THOMPKINS

Phillip, I'm taking the morning off to spend time with my wife. I would appreciate it if you would quit bothering me. If you have any questions, please ask Ashlyn. She has my full blessing to do whatever she sees fit.

PHILLIP

But Mayor Thompkins, she doesn't know what we do here. How can I trust her?"

MAYOR THOMPKINS

Remember that it's your job to do as I ask.

PHILLIP

I realize that, sir, but ...

MAYOR THOMPKINS

Then please just do your job.

I may have gone a little bit far with the last response, but Phillip Bane is the most annoying person I have ever met. Being that I mostly work for entitled movies stars, that's saying a lot.

Now that I've told Phillip my dad is spending the morning with my mom, I have some time to kill before coming back to the office with his car. I decide to go to the library and do a deep dive into Maple Falls' history to see if I can come up with something that will help us.

CHAPTER 16
JAMIE

PRACTICE GOES WELL, and I'm happily surprised by the natural chemistry our team seems to have on the ice. So far, no one is hogging the puck, and they're passing to everyone like they're trying to learn each other's strengths and weaknesses. If we continue like this, we might just be a contender for the Stanley, after all.

As soon as practice ends, Dale calls us all over. "I'm impressed and I don't say that lightly. We've got a lot of talent here and even though our season hasn't started, I'm proud of you all. Let's keep up the good work."

The men seemingly puff their chests at the compliment. We might be pro athletes, but getting approval from our coach is always appreciated. Dale continues, "The press are very interested in us right now, and I want all of you to take as many interviews as you can. Don't talk about the bachelor auction yet, but talk up Maple Falls; talk up your new team; and please don't be shy about mentioning your personal lives. That's always a big hit with the fans."

As the guys skate off the ice, Dale tells me, "I got a call from *Hockey* magazine. They say you've been avoiding their reporter. Why is that?"

"All they want to do is talk about Allegra, Dale. I don't want to talk about her."

"It's done, Jamie. Allegra left you and you've both moved on. Just keep your chin up and don't let them know you're bothered."

"But it does bother me. It would be one thing if I were seeing someone else, but I'm not. So, I look like the loser who got left, and that's not an image I want to perpetuate."

Dale puts his arm around my shoulder before saying, "You need a new girlfriend."

I shake my head hard enough that he takes a step away to avoid getting head-butted. "No, I don't."

"You don't need a *real* girlfriend," he says while looking at me meaningfully.

My face scrunches up in confusion. "Do you want me to buy a big stuffed animal and tell everyone she's my new life partner?"

"No, son. I want you to find a nice girl and I want you to go out on a few dates. You don't have to pledge your undying love. You don't have to ask her to marry you. Just show the world you've moved on, too. It's as easy as that."

Nothing he just said is easy. I live in Maple Falls and while I'm sure there are single women here, I don't know any of them. And even if I did, I'm not about to put myself in the position of having someone else talk to the press about me. No, thank you.

Before I can make this clear, Dale tells me, "There's a reporter coming by in a few minutes. I told her you would give an interview."

My head starts to tingle like I'm going to have a stroke. "Dale …" I start to say, but he doesn't give me a chance to finish my thought.

"You're the captain of the team, Jamie. You are the leader. As such, you have to show everyone you're a team player. I just told all the guys *they* had to talk to the press, and so do *you*. There's no way out."

I nod my head once to let him know I've heard him, but I don't trust myself to speak. His last sentiment, "there's no way out," feels as much a threat as it is a fact. I am the captain. I do have to lead.

Once I'm back in the locker room, I hurry to change out of my gear and then I head to the press room. As expected, the reporter is waiting for me. A tallish woman wearing jeans and a blazer stands up and walks toward me. Crud, she's pretty. It's bad enough that I look like a joke for the world to see, but now I have to explain to an attractive woman that I'm not man enough to keep my girlfriend. Fun times.

She reaches out her hand toward me. "Emily Hough from *Hockey* magazine."

I shake her hand and respond, "Jamie Hayes."

"Thank you for agreeing to talk to me, Jamie. You're a hard man to get an interview with."

I don't bother explaining why that is. I'm sure she already knows. Leading the way to the press table, I sit down and gesture for her to do the same. "I'm really excited about the Ice Breakers," I tell her. "I'm happy to answer any questions you have about the team."

I don't care if Dale wants me to talk about my personal life, I want to make it clear to Emily that isn't why I'm here.

She pulls out her phone and puts it on the table between us. "Do you mind if I record this?"

I always hate being recorded, but I nod my head like a good boy. "Great," she says. Looking down at a pad of paper she's holding, she announces, "I hear that you and Allegra have broken up. Did that have anything to do with your decision to leave New York and come to Maple Falls?"

It had everything to do with my decision and I'm sure she knows that, or she wouldn't have asked the question. Yet, I refuse to take the bait. "I loved playing for New York," I tell her. "I loved living in New York." I feel the need to throw in, "It's my hometown."

"Which makes it so surprising you left." She stares at me like she's trying to perform a Vulcan mind meld on me. *That's right, I'm an old-school Star Trek fan.*

"Emily," I say before taking a big breath, hoping to lower my rising blood pressure. "I started my career with Dale Hauser. He taught me everything about this game. When I was offered the opportunity to work with him again, I couldn't pass it up."

She looks disappointed by my answer. "What about Allegra?"

I try to shrug off her question in the most nonchalant manner possible. "What about her?"

"Are you upset about the breakup? Are you hoping to win her back?"

There's no way I can avoid answering, so I take a beat to try to get my thoughts together before saying, "Allegra and I were a couple for three years. We both have very demanding careers that kept us apart a lot." She looks at me expectantly, so I add, "The distance just became too much."

"That's why you think she left you?"

"You'd have to ask her if you want to know her reason."

She flips a page in her notebook before telling me, "Oh, I did." Even though I don't really want to hear what my ex said, I know Emily isn't going to spare me. "Allegra says that she loved you very much but when she met Brett Tremaine, it was like a switch turned on—like she'd been waiting for him her whole life." She looks down at her notes briefly before adding, "Brett told me that when their eyes met it was like they recognized each other from another place and time."

That's such romanticized drivel, I want to vomit. I want to suggest that Brett probably told his three ex-wives the same thing, but I know that would only make me look pathetic. So, I offer, "I think it's great they found each other. I'm a real proponent of love."

Emily's eyes narrow slightly like she doesn't believe me.

Going right for the jugular, she asks, "Are you heartbroken, Jamie?"

This, right here, is why I hate the press. They won't rest until I act out the part of abandoned boyfriend. *Am I heartbroken?* Maybe I was right after it happened, but it's been four months. I've managed to cruise along the stages of grief pretty quickly, even though I did spend a good amount of time wallowing in self-pity.

I decide to throw her a bone in hopes she'll take it and back off. "I wasn't happy when Allegra broke up with me, but if she hadn't …" What in the world do I say now? I search my brain, trying to come up with a way to finish that sentence.

I pause long enough that Emily asks, "If she hadn't, what?"

I'm as shocked as she is when I open my mouth and tell her, "If she didn't, I would have never met my current girlfriend."

Emily looks all kinds of excited that she's the one who gets to break this news to the world. "What's her name? How long have you been seeing each other? Is she here in Maple Falls with you?"

All valid questions that I don't have the answer to because … wait for it … *I'm lying.* "We're not ready to make our relationship public yet," I tell her before asking, "Any chance you'll keep the information to yourself for now?"

She laughs loudly in response. "Sorry, Jamie, no. If you'd wanted to keep that on the down-low, you should have told me upfront."

Yeah, that's what I thought.

"Can you at least tell me something about her?" Emily asks hopefully.

And right here is where I completely lose it because the only woman who pops into my mind is the mayor's daughter. That's probably why I stupidly say, "I don't think Ashlyn would appreciate that."

"Ashlyn?" she asks excitedly. "Ashlyn what?"

I shift nervously in my seat. "I think I've told you enough."

"Does she live in Maple Falls?" she prods like a velociraptor on the Jurassic Park fence.

"No, she doesn't." At least that part's true. Ashlyn Thompkins lives in Los Angeles. She's only visiting Maple Falls.

"Is she here now?" Emily looks around wildly like my made-up girlfriend is going to jump out from behind some random piece of furniture.

I pick up my phone like I'm looking at the time, before announcing, "I'm running late for my next appointment." Then I stand up and tell her, "I appreciate your taking the time to talk to me." *More lies.*

She stands up as well. "I appreciate *you* taking the time to talk to *me*." Her grin is straight up cat after eating the canary. *Rather, a whole flock of them.* "I'll be on the lookout for your new girlfriend, Jamie."

I just bet she will. "If I promise to tell you who she is before I tell any other reporter, will you not look too hard?"

Her exaggerated snort says it all. My life is fair game and Emily is not going to cut me any slack.

CHAPTER 17
ASHLYN

THE FIRST THING I do when I get to the library is to search out old maps of Maple Falls. I need to find out exactly where Victor MacDonald's property was located. As I spread the first drawing out on an old walnut table, my knee strikes something sticky. *Gross.* I wonder how much gum has been stuck to the underside over the years. Maybe as acting mayor I can assign the task of cleaning off old gum to people who get caught littering. Or better yet, to Phillip.

Forcing myself to refocus, I scan the first map. According to the key on the copy of the original settlement boundaries map, everything marked in blue belonged to Victor MacDonald. My heart sinks into the pit of my stomach like a lead weight when I see blue everywhere.

Consulting a copy of Maple Falls' most recent map, I learn what property is at risk. An audible gasp escapes me when I see that it encompasses a large amount of Main Street, as well as the arena. Of less importance to the town, but of great importance to everyone on my parents' street, the preserve behind a lot of our homes is also under threat. *This is so, so bad.*

Taking both maps up to the librarian I ask him to please make copies for me. Once I have them, I go to my car and call

Phillip. He doesn't answer his phone, which I can only take to mean that he doesn't want to talk to me. *That makes two of us, buddy.*

I call Marcy next. Before she can say anything, I blurt out, "It's worse than we thought, Marcy."

"How bad is it?" she sounds nervous.

"Victor MacDonald owned the land the arena is on, as well as a big part of Main Street."

"No!"

"I'm guessing his heir knows this and he's going to play hardball. I mean, why wouldn't he?"

"Do you have an emergency meeting called yet?"

"I asked my dad's assistant to do it, but the guy hates me. I'm not overly optimistic he's going to make it happen." I slump back against the driver's seat and start to seriously consider calling my dad.

"I'll do it," Marcy says. "I have all the names and numbers of the council members. I'll set the meeting for tomorrow afternoon."

I exhale loudly. "I'm sure everyone will love being called in on a Sunday."

"At least most of them should be able to make it," Marcy says. "Are you sure you don't want to call your dad?"

"I'd like to see if I can't handle this before I do."

"I'll make the meeting for two o'clock. That way stomachs will be full, and hopefully brains will be ready to come up with some great ideas."

"Where does the town council meet?"

"There's a room on the first floor of Town Hall," she tells me. That makes sense even though I envisioned it in a quaint building in the middle of town like they used in that old television series, *Gilmore Girls.*

After hanging up with Marcy, I look at the clock. It's nearly eleven, so instead of driving my dad's car to the office, I text Phillip from his phone.

> MAYOR THOMPKINS
>
> I'm taking the day off to spend with Mrs. Thompkins. Don't worry about setting up the emergency meeting, Marcy Fontaine is taking care of that.

The ellipses appear immediately. So the little sneak *was* avoiding me.

> PHILLIP
>
> Sir, I was going to set up the meeting as soon as I spoke to you. Your daughter wouldn't tell me what it's about.

> MAYOR THOMPKINS
>
> Don't worry about it, Phillip. Ashlyn is on it.

> PHILLIP
>
> But, sir ...

I don't bother responding. I figure the less I pretend to be my dad, the better. It's bad enough I'll have to host the meeting tomorrow without the actual mayor being present, but I'll come up with some excuse.

Before I leave the library parking lot, I get another text. This time it's from Jamie Hayes.

> JAMIE
>
> I'm done at the rink. Is the offer to show me around town still open?

Shoot, I forgot about that. I suppose the good news is that Jamie knows what's going on with Victor MacDonald's land so he can help me brainstorm.

> ME
>
> How about if we meet at the farmers' market? It's at the park at the edge of town.

JAMIE

That's not very specific. Isn't there an address
or something?

ME

Just follow the crowd.

JAMIE

Are you serious?

ME

Jamie, this is Maple Falls, not New York. Trust
me, you really can't miss it.

On the way to the market, the gravity of what's happening
hits me. My hometown is in serious jeopardy. I'm just grateful
my dad will be home next week, and he'll be able to take over.
All I have to do is get the ball rolling and then I can go back to
LA and my own life.

The parking lot around the farmers' market is packed, so I
have to park a good distance from the entrance. I see several
people I know on the way in. Some of them I simply wave to,
but others, like Bailey, I stop to chat with. I'm also eyeing her
delicious-looking maple butter products she's carrying in for her
booth.

When I finally arrive at the entrance, I spot Jamie waiting for
me. He's talking to two young boys that I don't know. Hurrying
to his side, I tell him, "Sorry it took me so long. I bumped into
half the town in the parking lot."

"No worries," he says before turning his attention back to the
boys. "I'll be looking for you two at the arena, okay?" They nod
enthusiastically before running away. "Two of Troy Hart's boys,"
he tells me.

Before we can walk in, a woman about my age runs over to
us. I'm half-convinced she's going to hit us bowling-ball style,
but she slows down at the last minute. "Jamie!" she calls out.

The look on my new friend's face suggests she's someone

he's not happy to see. "A fan?" I guess. The interloper arrives before he can answer.

"Emily," he says to her. "What are you doing here?"

"I followed you from the arena." *Hmm, maybe she's a stalker.*

"I wish you wouldn't have." He steps in front of me like he's trying to shield me.

The woman looks around him right at me and asks, "Ashlyn?"

"Do I know you?" Just because I don't recognize her doesn't mean we didn't go to school together or something. People do change.

She looks so happy, I'm convinced we must have been best friends at some point. "You're Ashlyn, right?" she repeats.

I step around Jamie and tell her, "Ashlyn Thompkins. Did you go to Maple Falls High?"

She shakes her head. "I'm a reporter for *Hockey* magazine. I have a couple of questions for you, if you don't mind."

How in the world did the press get ahold of the Victor MacDonald story already? I've only known about it for a day. "Did Alexander MacDonald contact you?" I ask, sounding a bit more hostile than I intended.

"Who's that?" she asks.

Well, if she doesn't know, I'm sure as heck not going to tell her. "No one," I mumble before asking, "What could you possibly want to talk to me about?"

"Jamie Hayes," she says excitedly.

The color drains from Jamie's face. "Please, Emily, I told you I'm not ready to talk about this publicly yet."

"That doesn't mean Ashlyn isn't," she says with a near-maniacal grin on her face.

My head swivels between the two of them. "Ready to talk about what?"

Jamie agitatedly says, "Nothing. There's nothing to talk about."

At the same time, Emily states, "I want to ask you about your relationship with Jamie. He claims he's not ready to share that you're his new girlfriend, but seeing as you're standing right here, I figure you might have something you'd like to say."

"His new what, now?" I want to know.

"His new girlfriend," she repeats.

"I'm not his ..." before I can say "girlfriend," Jamie takes my arm and starts to pull me away from her.

Then he says loudly, "Come on, honey. You don't need to talk to the press. Our relationship is none of their business."

What in the world is he talking about?

CHAPTER 18
JAMIE

"WHAT'S GOING ON?" Ashlyn asks me while skipping to keep up with my determined stride.

I take two more steps before stopping. Then I look around to see if Emily is following us. When I don't see her, I gently take Ashlyn's elbow and lead her to a nearby bench. Once we're seated, I confess, "I made a huge mistake."

When I don't start explaining myself right away, she prompts, "Go on."

Sighing dramatically, I tell her, "I've been avoiding the press ever since Allegra left me. All they want to do is dig up dirt and make me look like a jilted fool. I want no part of that."

"I suppose they're just doing their job," she says like that somehow makes it okay to drag me over the coals.

"Right." Running my hands through my hair, I tell her, "Dale set up the meeting with Emily, and as expected, she did her best to make me look pathetic."

"So, you told her you were dating me?" She doesn't sound pleased.

"I told her I had a new girlfriend. I might have mentioned her name was Ashlyn, but only because your name was the first one to pop into my head."

"Are you asking me out?" Her tone can only be construed as horrified. *How unflattering.*

"Not at all," I assure her. "But I don't suppose you'd be willing to go along with the charade until you go back to Los Angeles?" I feel like a hopeful puppy waiting for a bone. Or at the very least, a pat on the head.

Ashlyn is quiet for so long I'm sure she's going to say no. But then she asks, "What would being your fake girlfriend entail?"

I hurry to tell her, "You would have to be seen with me occasionally. I would pay for everything, of course. And whatever you want on top of that."

Her eyes glitter with excitement. "Are we talking shopping sprees here?"

"I suppose." Up until this point, Ashlyn has not struck me as that kind of woman, but I don't really know her well. If she wants to shop, I can get behind that.

"Just kidding," she laughs. "What I really want is for you to agree to be part of the bachelor auction."

She sounds so hopeful, I'm tempted to tell her the truth, that I've already been ordered to step up on the auction block. Yet, I don't feel it's in my best interest to share this piece of information. "I would absolutely participate in the auction."

Her smile is radiant, and I feel an unwelcome stirring in my chest. I remind myself that I'm not really going to be dating Ashlyn. If being with Allegra taught me anything, it's that there are enough complications in relationships that you shouldn't go out of your way to look for more. And Ashlyn living in LA is a giant complication.

"If you do the auction," Ashlyn crosses her legs before facing me head on, "I'll be your fake girlfriend."

I'm so relieved I want to jump up and shout at the rooftops. But then an image from that old Oprah episode pops into my head. You know, the one where Tom Cruise did the same thing while confessing his love for Katie Holmes? On top of everything else going on, I cannot be portrayed as that much of a fool, so I sit still.

"Thank you, Ashlyn. You don't know what this means to me."

"You're doing me a huge favor as well," she tells me. "Any chance I can get you to come to the emergency town meeting tomorrow? It might lessen some nerves knowing that we have the Ice Breakers on our side. Especially being that … well …"

"What?" I ask nervously.

Her body slumps noticeably against the back of the bench. "I just went to the library and looked up the original map of Maple Falls. The entire arena is on Victor MacDonald's property."

"What does that mean for the Ice Breakers?"

She shrugs. "I don't know what any of this means. A big part of downtown was his, as well. There are now a bunch of businesses that could be in real trouble."

"I'll see if Dale and Troy Hart can come too." It looks like the future of the Ice Breakers could be in real jeopardy, and that's honestly the last thing I need.

"Thank you," Ashlyn says.

"What does your dad say about all this?" I ask her. It suddenly occurs to me that I seem super involved for someone who doesn't even live here.

"My dad?"

"Yes." I smile. "You might know him as the mayor?"

Ashlyn looks from left to right. Then she stares right at me. "I've agreed to be your fake girlfriend, right?"

"Right …"

"So, if I tell you something, you have to keep it to yourself."

I have no idea what she's going to say, but a burst of anxiety hits me square in the chest. "Of course."

She moves closer before whispering, "My dad is out of town with my mom."

"And?" I'm not sure why that's such a big secret. People do go away.

She leans even closer. "My parents' marriage is on the rocks and the only way I could get my dad to agree to try to fix it was to promise I wouldn't tell anyone he's gone. If he found out what was happening, he'd come right home. Then my parents' marriage would end."

"He'd pick the town over your mom?"

"He thinks he's the supreme ruler of Maple Falls," she says. "I had to take his phone so he would concentrate on my mother and not spend the entire time calling people here."

"And no one can know he's not in Maple Falls?" My brain races at the thought of the kind of deception Ashlyn is perpetrating.

"I thought that was kind of silly at first too, but now that the town is in real trouble, it wouldn't look good if people knew the mayor wasn't coming to the rescue. Better they think he's hard at work trying to solve the situation."

"So, you're doing your dad's job and when anyone asks for him you're pretending he's off playing superhero somewhere else? What will they think when he's not at the meeting tomorrow night?"

She shrugs. "I haven't had time to think about that yet, but I'll come up with something."

"Wow, okay. Can I tell Dale and Troy?"

She shakes her head. "Don't tell anyone. Marcy Fontaine is the only other person who knows."

"Who's she?" I ask.

"She's Maple Falls' accountant."

This is starting to feel like some kind of crazy slapstick comedy. *The mayor's daughter, an accountant, and a hockey player come together to save a small town in Washington from the evil antagonist who is trying to ruin them.* Talk about unrealistic. "How about if we find a place here to have lunch?" I suggest. "Or if you prefer, we could go into town."

She stands up excitedly. "Let's stay here. Not only is the farmers' market a big part of our town's culture, but they have a pretzel booth that makes the most amazing sandwiches you'll ever eat. Oh, and my mom has been telling me about a girl named Neesha who sells, and I quote, 'the best cupcakes in the world.' I could sure go for one of those."

"That sounds great," I tell her as my stomach rumbles in anticipation.

Ashlyn leads the way, and we walk through the various stands selling their early fall goods. There are lots of pumpkins, winter squash, and root vegetables galore. As we pass a booth with floral bouquets, I stop and buy the biggest one they have. The blooms are vibrant orange, red, and yellow.

After paying for the arrangement, I hand it to Ashlyn. "Thank you for agreeing to help me."

She glances behind me as she takes the bouquet. Then she steps closer to me and whispers, "Emily is watching us, and she has her phone pointed in our direction."

"Looks like she'll get a nice picture of me giving my girl-friend flowers, then." I'm having such a good time, I don't even mind.

Ashlyn smiles coyly. "Yes, she will. But if you want me to act like your *real* girlfriend, I should probably do this ..." Standing on her tiptoes, she gives me the briefest and sweetest kiss, right on the mouth.

She did not have to do that, and I'm touched she's taking her role so seriously. I try to find the words to express my gratitude, but I'm struck mute. Reaching out, I take Ashlyn's free hand and walk toward the sign for pretzel sandwiches.

Ashlyn Thompkins is an unexpected person in my life, and if I'm not careful, I could lose my heart to her.

CHAPTER 19
ASHLYN

WHAT IN THE world was I thinking kissing Jamie yesterday? The truth is, I wasn't thinking. I got swept away in the romance of being gifted a beautiful bunch of flowers. I thought I could handle a fake boyfriend, but it turns out I'm going to have to remind myself the whole thing is just for show. The problem is, whenever I remember the softness of Jamie's lips and the minty heat of his breath, I turn to mush. Which is not how a fake girl-friend should be feeling.

I like Jamie Hayes a lot. He's sweet, he cares about others, and he truly is a team player. It's no wonder he was chosen to be the captain of the Ice Breakers. But even so, he's not for me. As much as I joke about having to move to Utah to find a man, I am not going to date a guy who doesn't even live in the same city as I do. There are enough obstacles in life without adding that one.

I hurriedly brush my hair and tie it back in a ponytail. Then I put on a jean skirt and pair it with a rust-colored cashmere sweater that sets off the highlights in my hair. I may not look professional like a mayor should, but as far as the town knows, I'm just the mayor's daughter and nothing else. Except that I'm conducting an emergency meeting, instead of the man they voted into office. *Gah, I need to come up with a credible story, fast!*

On the drive to Town Hall, my head is bursting trying to figure out how to tell everyone what's going on. It's going to be one of those pivotal moments where one minute, life is normal and good, and the next, everyone's apple cart gets toppled like a Real Housewife flipping over a dinner table. Side note: I was hired to arrange said housewife's closet for her and she's just as terrifying in person as she is on television.

Phillip is once again standing in the parking lot in the middle of my dad's space. I don't even pretend to slow down this time. I just speed up and give him the scare of his life.

He jumps to the sidewalk before shouting, "Why did you do that?"

Getting out of my car, I storm past him with determination. "I have a meeting to conduct, Phillip."

"Where is your dad? Why are you even here?" He has to run to keep up with me, and I'm suddenly tempted to stick a foot out and trip him.

I still haven't decided what to tell people about my father's absence, so instead of answering his question, I walk even faster. As soon as I'm inside the building, I find the meeting room and scurry inside.

Even though I'm early, I'm not the first one here. I see Mike Mitchell and Elaine Fishman who, according to the list Marcy texted me, are both members of the town council. There are seven members—six council people and the mayor.

Elaine Fishman hurries over to me and asks, "Ashlyn, what are you doing home?" It's surprising how many times I've heard this question. You'd think people would expect me to visit once in a while. I mean, I did grow up here.

"Hi, Mrs. Fishman." I tell her, "I'm home to see my folks. You know there's nothing quite like fall in the Pacific Northwest."

"You should have come for Maple Fest then, dear. Surely you're not staying long enough for that?"

Being that Maple Fest is nearly a month away, I am not staying. "You know how it is, Mrs. Fishman. I travel in between jobs, so I don't miss work."

She pats my hand. "I understand, dear. Now where's your father? I can't help but wonder why he needed to bring us all in on a Sunday." She's still wearing her church clothes, which means she probably left a roast in the oven to come here.

"He's um, rather ..." Jamie saves me by walking in. He's with two other men who I assume are his coach and the Ice Breakers' owner, Troy Hart. "Mrs. Fishman, if you'll excuse me, I need to go talk to someone."

"Yes, well, I suppose, but ..."

I rush over to Jamie. "Thanks for coming." Tingles of awareness fill my nervous system as I catch a whiff of his clove-scented cologne. I just kissed this man yesterday, and so help me, I'd like to do it again.

Jamie gestures toward the friendly looking middle-aged man on his right and introduces him, "Ashlyn, this is my coach, Dale Hauser." Then he turns to his other side and adds, "This is Troy Hart."

I shake both men's hands before telling them, "I appreciate your coming. I'm guessing Jamie has filled you in on what's happened."

Troy is the first to speak. "I'm more than a little concerned about this. I have a bill of sale for the arena, and it includes the twelve acres surrounding it."

"I know, Mr. Hart. A lot of businesses are affected."

"Are all the owners coming today?" Dale wants to know.

I shake my head. "I wanted to keep this small so we could come up with a preliminary plan before getting everyone riled up."

"Oh, they're going to get riled," Troy says. "How could they not, with their livelihoods at stake?"

"Why don't we all go sit down," I suggest.

After the rest of the council members have arrived and we

take our seats, Phillip walks into the room and demands, "Where is Mayor Thompkins?"

Councilman Mitchell echoes, "Yes, where *is* the mayor? I don't know about everyone else, but I had plans with my family this afternoon and I'm curious why we've been summoned. This is highly unusual."

Standing up, I address the group. "Most of you know that I'm Mayor Thompkins' daughter, Ashlyn." After a few grunts and greetings, I continue, "My dad isn't feeling very well today. He's asked me to make his apologies for being unable to attend. I'm here in his place."

"What do you mean he's not coming?" Phillip raises his fists like he's carrying a torch and leading a pack of rioting townsfolk. "I talked to him myself and he said he'd meet me here. He never mentioned feeling unwell."

First off, Phillip never spoke to my dad. He's just saying this so he can look important, which is pitiful. Secondly, Phillip is a turd, and I want to smack him. "I don't know when you talked to my dad, Phillip, but he's been sick all morning. He thinks he might have food poisoning."

"Oh, dear." Mrs. Fishman's face collapses in concern. "I hope he didn't get it anywhere local."

"I'm sure he'll let the establishment know if it's food poisoning," I tell her. "Now, as to the reason we're all here." I look around the table meaningfully before announcing, "Victor MacDonald's heir has come forth and is demanding the return of his ancestor's property."

Councilman Mitchell bangs the table loudly with his fist. "That property was turned over to the city decades ago when an heir couldn't be found!"

"That's correct, Mr. Mitchell. But in the state of Washington there is no statute of limitations in an inheritance claim. Therefore, if Alexander MacDonald can prove he's the rightful heir, the property is legally his."

"How do we know this isn't all a hoax?" another council member calls out.

"I've been in touch with the claimant's lawyer, and he's promised to send documentation," I tell them.

Excited chatter erupts like I just announced the next winter Olympics are going to take place in our town. I call out, "If you'll please quiet down a moment, I'd like to tell you what our plan is."

Once the room settles, I explain, "My father feels the best way to deal with this is for Maple Falls to raise enough money to offer to buy the land from the current Mr. MacDonald."

"How much are we talking about?" Councilman Mitchell demands.

"There are five hundred acres, and we'd like to offer five thousand dollars an acre." The murmuring starts again, so I hurry to add, "Which may not be enough, being that the arena is also on that property. If Mr. MacDonald is hoping to capitalize on the Ice Breakers, we may have to come up with more."

I gesture toward Jamie, Troy, and Dale. "We have representatives here from the Ice Breakers who are going to start us off by hosting a bachelor auction."

Mrs. Fishman's eyes practically bug out of her head. "We're going to sell men?" She sounds more excited than disturbed by the idea. I look at her closely to see if I read her reaction right. *Yup, she's practically salivating.*

"The Ice Breakers are getting a lot of media attention these days, Mrs. Fishman, so we're hoping to bring in big dollars from outside Maple Falls for this."

Councilman Dryer, who used to be my dentist when I was a kid, raises his hand. "You think we can raise over two mil selling hockey players?"

"Again, Dr. Dryer, we're not selling them. We're merely renting them for an evening."

Coach Hauser calls out, "A couple of hours, tops."

Jamie inserts, "Forty-five minutes."

I wave them both off. "We'll work out the particulars later. But no, Dr. Dryer, we are not going to make all the money with this one endeavor. We're going to need the town's participation. That's why we're here—to brainstorm fundraising ideas, as well as to figure out how to tell everyone what's going on."

Anxiety is clearly running high, which makes me glad we started small and didn't invite the whole town right off the bat. That would have been a huge circus.

In the end, we decide the best way to share this information is through the local newspaper. That way people can read the facts, and the story won't alter between tellings. That's not to say folks won't gossip and start adding to the tale, but at least there will be something on record to support the truth.

"What if the heir reads the story and finds out what we're doing? Won't that tip him off?" Mrs. Fishman wants to know.

Picking up a piece of paper, I fan it across my face. "He's going to find out anyway, Mrs. Fishman. I'm going to talk to his lawyer to see if he's even willing to consider an offer. In the meantime, we're going to start raising money in hopes that he will."

"And if he doesn't?" Phillip demands. "What then, Ashlyn?"

Inhaling deeply, I tell the room, "Then we'll find another way."

Staring at the various shocked faces around the table makes me feel like the grim reaper at a church potluck. It's hard to believe Maple Falls is facing such a horrible fate as having Alexander MacDonald come to town and change the very face of our existence.

Yet that's where we are, so we have no choice but to jump in and do everything in our power to come out on top.

CHAPTER 20
JAMIE

A HEAVY SENSE of dread hangs over the room as the town council meeting comes to an end. It's clear everyone is anxious, and I feel compelled to speak up. "I know this is a troubling situation, but Maple Falls is tough, and everyone is so community-minded. I know we will prevail."

Councilman Mitchell responds, "It's all well and good for *you* to think that, but it's not *your* town."

Dale interjects, "It is our town, Councilman Mitchell. My guys are going to live here for several months while we train and get through the season. That gives us a significant stake in a happy outcome for Maple Falls." He adds, "The last thing we need is having to find another arena at this late date."

Mrs. Fishman bats her eyes at me and asks, "Are you going to be for sale, Jamie?"

"I ... um ... rather ..." I don't like the way she's looking at me—like I'm the biggest and gooiest chocolate chip cookie she's ever seen, and the bakery just announced I was the last one left.

Before I can answer her, Dale says, "All of my single players will be participating in the auction, Mrs. Fishman." He glances at Ashlyn before adding, "Bidding will start at five thousand dollars."

Undeterred, Mrs. Fishman winks at me. "Good thing I invested in bitcoin back when it was only dollars."

As everyone stands up to leave the meeting, there's still a sense of unfinished business in the air. Troy walks up to me and says, "I'm going to promote the heck out of this bachelor auction. We should be able to get a lot of wealthy women and celebrities to come for the publicity alone. We really can't have the season upset by having to relocate everyone."

Even though the thought nauseates me, I tell him, "Sounds good." Now that Ashlyn is pretending to be my girlfriend, I'm hoping she'll bid on me. I'll give her whatever amount of money she needs to make that happen.

"What about you, Dale? Are you going to get in on the action?" Troy asks.

My coach tips his head from side-to-side uncertainly. "I wouldn't mind doing it, but I don't want to be the only guy there to go for twenty bucks."

Troy laughs. "If that's all you get, then I'll up the bid to forty."

Dale rolls his eyes. "Thanks. That'll do wonders for my ego."

After saying goodbye to the council members, Ashlyn joins us. "I'm going to stay and draft an article for the newspaper. Is there anything you all would like me to add regarding the Ice Breakers?"

"Just make sure to mention how happy we are to be in Maple Falls," Troy tells her. "And that we're excited to do whatever is needed to save our town."

Nodding her head, Ashlyn turns to me. "Do you want to stay and help, Jamie?"

"You bet he does!" This comes from Dale. "Our captain will be happy to lend assistance. Isn't that right, Jamie?"

Ashlyn glances at me out of the corner of her eye so I nod my head to let her know I'm good with it.

After Troy and Dale leave, some guy wearing a sweater vest storms over to us. Beads of sweat dot his forehead like he just ran a mile. "I don't know what you're up to, Ashlyn, but I know something is going on here and I'm going to get to the bottom of it."

Ashlyn glares at him menacingly, before saying, "Bite the wall, Phillip."

"Well, I never!" he responds.

"There's a reason for that," Ashlyn murmurs. Then she turns her back on him and asks me, "Should we sit down?"

"I'm going to stay, too," Phillip says.

Touching Ashlyn's arm to get her attention, I suggest, "Let's go somewhere else. I'll drive."

"I'm going to call the mayor!" Phillip shouts. But neither Ashlyn nor I respond. We simply walk out of the room.

Once we're in the hall outside, I ask her, "Who was that guy?"

"Phillip Bane, my father's assistant," she hisses.

"He's pretty intense."

"He wants to be mayor after my dad's term is up and he's afraid I'm going to be competition. As if I would ever want to be the mayor of Maple Falls." She clearly finds that prospect distasteful.

As we exit the building, I point to my car parked by the curb. "Should we have lunch in town?"

Ashlyn shakes her head. "The council members are probably spreading the word as we speak. I don't want to have to answer a bunch of questions until people read the newspaper article."

"I have frozen meals at my place," I tell her. "How does that sound?"

"Disgusting. Why don't we get takeout from the Glass Olive? Their eggplant parmesan is the best I've ever had."

I open the passenger door for Ashlyn. Once we're both inside, we look up the menu for the restaurant. After calling in our order, I ask her, "How are you feeling?"

"Terrified," she confesses. "I so badly want to call my dad for advice, but I know he'll come running."

I reach out and give her forearm a brief squeeze of encouragement. "Your dad couldn't do anything that you're not already doing." I itemize, "You located the boundaries of the disputed land, you've held an emergency meeting to let the town leaders know what's going on, and you've put the ball in motion for a bachelor auction. You've done a lot, Ashlyn. You've got this."

She looks over at me with gratitude. "I couldn't have done it without your help. Thank you."

I hate having her think I'm the good guy here, so I tell her, "Dale was already making me do the bachelor auction before you asked."

Her eyebrows nearly hit her hairline in surprise. "So you're not doing it so I'll pretend to be your girlfriend?"

I shake my head slowly. "You don't have to pretend to be my girlfriend anymore if you don't want to."

"Why did you confess this to me?"

"I … well …" *Why does this woman make it so hard for me to think clearly?* I finally manage to tell her, "You're an impressive woman, Ashlyn. You're trying to help your parents and your hometown, and you're doing it all selflessly." I add, "I'd like to be your friend, and I don't think friends should lie to each other."

"No one should lie," she says. Then out of nowhere, she asks, "Are you still in love with your ex?"

I should tell her that I'm not. After all, how could I love someone who treated me so badly? But I can't seem to utter those words. "We were together for three years. That's a long time to care about someone."

"But she left you," Ashlyn says, like I need reminding.

"She did. But the truth is that I probably didn't make as much time for us as I should have. It takes two to have a successful relationship."

"So, you do love her?"

Shrugging, I tell her, "Part of me will always love her. But that doesn't mean I want her back."

"Love is complicated, isn't it?" Ashlyn asks. "I'm sorry you're going through such a tough time." She actually sounds sincere.

"Thank you. Now let's go get our lunch so we can get back to my place and write this article."

Once we have our food, and are on the way to my temporary home, Ashlyn asks, "How are you doing with the bears?"

"The mama and the baby are fine, but the papa hates my guts."

She giggles. "You're going to need to let him know you're not a threat. The way you scream when you see him probably has him on edge."

Turning into the driveway, I tell her, "I don't scream."

"Uh-huh."

"I made a loud noise like I was told to." Her smile is so endearing, I can't help but relent. "Fine, I screamed. But you'll have to agree, that *is* a loud noise."

After putting the car in park, I turn off the ignition and pick up the bags of our food. "You ready to go?"

"Oh, I'm ready. The question is, are you?" She jumps out of the car like there's no potential threat lurking.

I open the driver's side door slowly before joining her. Looking around, I say, "It looks like the coast is clear." Then I practically run up to the cabin.

Ashlyn takes her time.

"Hurry up," I tell her nervously. Just because we don't see the papa bear doesn't mean he isn't waiting behind a tree. Or, god forbid, hiding in the branches above, primed to drop down like some crazy ninja bear.

When Ashlyn finally joins me on the porch, she says, "You really aren't suited for life in small town Washington, are you?"

"There's not much I can do about it now," I tell her. "I'm stuck here during the season, so I'm going to have to make the best of it." That's when I hear the papa bear announce his presence. Instinct takes over and before I can stop myself, I scream once again.

It's a good thing nothing more than friendship can ever happen between me and Ashlyn, because at the rate I'm going, I probably don't have a man-card left.

CHAPTER 21
ASHLYN

MAPLE FALLS MUST BE one of the only towns left on the planet where most people still subscribe to the newspaper. Opening the front door of my parents' house, I retrieve their copy of the *Gazette* before bringing it back inside.

I contacted the editor of the paper yesterday and filled him in on what's happening. He asked for a letter to the town from my father. He said that if he got it by six, he would go into the office and reconfigure the Monday edition. We got it to him at five fifty-eight.

Sitting down in the breakfast nook in the kitchen, I open the newspaper and discover we've made the front page.

Dear Citizens of Maple Falls,

It is with a heavy heart that I need to inform you about a situation that has developed in our town.

My office received a call a couple of days ago from an attorney who represents Victor MacDonald's heir. According to documents sent, Alexander MacDonald's daughter, Alexa, was working on a project regarding her family tree. By utilizing FamilyHeritage.com, she discovered her family was directly connected to Victor MacDonald. After doing some research, she learned about the sizable amount of unclaimed land that was left behind by her relative.

As Washington state does not have a statute of limitations on inheritances, we are no longer the owners of Victor's land. Several properties in our downtown area, the entire arena and outlying land, as well as preservation sites are affected.

In an emergency town council meeting held yesterday, we brainstormed ideas to raise the amount of money needed to hopefully buy back this land. For the five hundred acres, we are looking to raise two and a half million dollars. While this is a daunting sum, we are confident our town can make it happen.

The first idea decided upon was to hold a bachelor auction with our newly-minted NHL team, the Ice Breakers. Both Troy Hart, the owner of the team and arena, along with Dale Hauser, the team's coach, were present. They were joined by team captain Jamie Hayes. The Ice Breakers assured us that they are one hundred percent behind Maple Falls and will do everything in their power to help.

The bachelor auction will be held on October 24th. While we anticipate it bringing in a good amount of money, we also need our townsfolk to participate in any way they can. This is a grassroots effort, so nothing is too small. We're talking about bake sales, car washes, crafting events. Whatever you can do to help, this is your call to arms!

Maple Falls needs all its citizens to step up and fight for our future.

Please join us at our regularly scheduled town hall meeting on October 3rd and bring your ideas.

Very Sincerely,
Mayor Thompkins

I've barely finished reading the letter when my dad's phone rings. I'm not surprised to see that it's Phillip.

After sending the call to voicemail, I finish my cup of coffee before going upstairs to change. Then I collect a couple of items that will hopefully help get me through the day.

Before leaving the house, I call my mom to see how she's doing. She answers on the third ring. "Hey, Mom, how are things?" I ask, trying to sound relaxed.

"It's very beautiful here, Ashlyn," she says. "You did a nice job in choosing a location."

"Have you heard about the hurricane?"

"We have."

"And?"

"It doesn't look like it will hit us directly. They're only expecting heavy showers. Having spent our whole lives in Washington, I think we can handle that."

"How's Dad doing?"

"Your father is surprisingly present. We're having a good time."

"Have you heard any local news about Maple Falls?" I ask.

"Only the fourteen messages from various people regarding the letter from your dad in this morning's paper. I'm telling everyone the mayor knows what he's doing and that all will be well."

"And by the mayor, you mean me?"

"Exactly."

"I don't know what I'm doing, Mom," I tell her, all the while wondering why she has such confidence in me. "And Phillip is driving me crazy trying to get to Dad."

"He's an annoying man," she confirms.

"I don't think he's going to lighten up. He's very concerned that he hasn't spoken to the mayor directly. Is there any way you can record Dad saying a couple things for me so I can use them to appease Phillip?"

"I could try …" She doesn't sound convincing.

"Please, Mom. I really need this."

"What would you like me to get your father to say?"

I think for a moment before giving her a list.

"That's a lot."

"I may not need them all, but I've got to get this guy to settle down. Please do your best." I add, "You know, like I'm doing my best to help you and Dad?"

"Yes, dear. I know you're very supportive. I'll try to be the same. In the meantime, tell Phillip you're going to start bringing your pet snake into work. He hates snakes."

"So do I," I assure her.

"Yes, but Phillip will cry if he sees a snake."

"And you know this how?"

My mom giggles. "His mother told me. She said that when Phillip was fifteen, he saw a garter snake in their yard, and he cried like a baby. She had to get him therapy."

I share Phillip's phobia, so I'm a little torn here. Even so, I put this piece of information in my back pocket in case of emergency. "Okay, Mom. I'm heading into the office now. Pray for me. I expect it's going to be an awful day."

Seemingly unconcerned with what lies ahead for me, she announces, "I had a mimosa with brunch. It was delightful, but I think I might need to take a nap to sleep it off."

"Please get Dad to record those things first."

"Bye, dear!" My mom hangs up so abruptly I start to wonder if she didn't have quite a few mimosas with brunch.

As I leave the house, I make a last-minute decision to take my dad's car to work in hopes it will convince Phillip that the mayor is in the building somewhere doing his best to save Maple Falls.

I just have to park it without him seeing that it's me behind the wheel.

A block away from Town Hall, I pull over and text my dad's assistant from his phone.

> MAYOR THOMPKINS
>
> Phillip, I'm on my way into the office. Will you please put on a fresh pot of coffee and make sure to have a cup on my desk waiting for me?

> PHILLIP
>
> Yes, sir! I'm glad you're feeling well enough to come into work. The town really needs you!

> MAYOR THOMPKINS
>
> Are you in the office now?

> PHILLIP
>
> I'm in the parking lot, sir. I'm waiting to greet you.

That slimy little slug of a sneak. I know he isn't there to greet my dad. He's trying to keep me from parking in my dad's spot.

> MAYOR THOMPKINS
>
> Hurry along inside, Phillip. My head hurts and I need my caffeine fix.

My dad's morning caffeine fix is something he talks about often, so I'm pretty sure his assistant will do as he's told.

Pulling back out onto the street, I turn into the parking lot. Sure, enough, I see the backside of Phillip walking into Town Hall. I hurry to pull into my dad's space. Once I'm out of the car, I text Phillip again.

> MAYOR THOMPKINS
>
> Phillip, I forgot a stack of papers in the front seat of my car. Can you please bring those in for me?

PHILLIP

Yes, sir!

I hide behind a bush long enough for Phillip to leave the building again, and then while his back is turned, I rush to the elevator, which is where I am when he next texts.

PHILLIP

There are no papers in your car, sir.

MAYOR THOMPKINS

Shoot. I'll text Ashlyn and ask her to bring them in with her. Sorry to bother you.

PHILLIP

No bother. I'm on my way up, sir. I'm looking forward to seeing you.

I hurry into my dad's office and open the door to his private bathroom—which is a pretty darn fancy feature for a small-town mayor's office. I prop his favorite toy onto the counter before shutting the door.

Within moments, Phillip barges into the office. He looks positively wild-eyed when he sees me instead of my dad. "What are you doing here?" he demands.

"What's it to you?"

"Your father said you were still at home. I just talked to him." Again, with the "I just talked to him." Does this moron know that talking and texting are two very different animals?

"I left before he did," I tell him. "I wasn't sure he was feeling up to coming in." Pointing at the bathroom door, I add, "And sure enough, I think it was too soon."

I hit the button on the toy's remote that I'm holding under the desk. The resulting sound is so funny it's all I can do not to burst into laughter. One short toot is followed by a cluster and then a long, rattling chain of flatulence.

Phillip stops short in front of the door like he's afraid a bomb might go off. Then he yells out, "Sir, are you okay?"

I hit the fart machine's remote again which starts a different variation of sounds.

Phillip turns toward me in shock. Trying not to howl with laughter at Phillip's face, I insist, "I told him he wasn't well enough to come in, but he wouldn't listen."

"What's wrong with him? Do you still think it's food poisoning?"

"I'm worried it's the flu. I hope you've had your flu shot, Phillip."

The panic etched across his face is truly satisfying. "I haven't had it yet."

"Maybe you should go do that now," I suggest.

"But if the mayor has the flu, getting a shot now won't help me. It takes a couple of weeks to build up the antibodies needed to ward off contamination."

I give him my best deadpan glare. "Maybe you should plan on spending some time at home then. You know, just to be safe."

Phillip looks conflicted. It's clear he doesn't want to leave me here without him, but he also wants to stay healthy. He takes one step toward the bathroom door, so I click the remote again. This time a long and rumbling serenade explodes from the speaker and echoes off the walls of the small room.

Phillip turns around and practically sprints toward the door leading out of the office. "I think I will go get my flu shot. Please tell your father I'll continue to stay on top of things from home."

And just like that, my day gets easier. Now all I have to do is contact Alexander MacDonald's lawyer and see if he thinks his client might be willing to sell back his land to Maple Falls at the bargain basement price of two and a half million dollars.

CHAPTER 22
JAMIE

I HAVE two appointments to see houses with a realtor today. She originally had five places to show me, but three of them backed up against the woods. As I'm not willing to risk life and limb living near bears, I passed on those.

As soon as I'm safely in my car, I call Ashlyn. "Any chance you want to look at some houses?" I ask.

"Are you renting or buying?" she wants to know.

"Does it matter?"

"If you're buying, I'm coming."

"But not if I'm renting?" I'm confused.

"Buying is a bigger commitment, and I could have some insights you might need. If you're renting you're not liable for problems so it's not such a big deal."

"What kind of insights?"

"For instance, I don't want you buying a house where some horrible crime took place."

She's making me nervous. "Are there many of those? Because that is not the way Maple Falls was sold to me."

"There's a house on Church Street that's for sale. I got my first kiss there," she says.

"And that was a crime somehow?" I'm eager to hear this tale.

She laughingly tells me, "Yes it was, because I never got a second one from Billy Trinkle. After kissing me, he developed a mad crush on my friend Melissa and started dating her."

"Right up there with treason then, huh?"

"Exactly. And as your fake girlfriend, you really can't support that kind of offense."

Ashlyn is adorably funny, and the more I get to know her, the more I'm surprised some smart man hasn't seen what a catch she is and begged her to marry him. "But if it had worked out with Billy," I tell her, "You might not have been single today to be my fake girlfriend."

"Correct," she says. "So, you see why you can't buy that house."

Not at all, but I don't say that. "To answer your question," I tell her, "I'm planning to buy so I'm going to need you. Want me to come in and get you?"

"That would be great. If anyone asks what you're doing here, tell them you have an appointment with the mayor."

"Anyone other than Phillip giving you a hard time about your dad's disappearance?"

"Not yet. I either tell people they just missed him, or I send them on a wild goose chase to the coffee room. So far, so good."

I reach for my jacket and put it on. "Sneaky. I'll see you soon."

Peering out the front door, I look to see if I have any company. Sure enough, I spot the male bear standing to the left of the porch. It's like he's on constant sentry duty and that's his assigned post. Well, shoot, I can't leave now.

Going into the kitchen, I search the cabinets for something I can throw to divert him. I know Ashlyn said not to feed the bears, but food is the only thing I can think of that might buy me a few moments of safety to get to my car. I grab the first thing I see which is a box of granola.

Once I'm on the porch, I chuck the whole thing into the trees behind the bear. As soon as he turns, I run to my car and get in. I really need to find a house today. One that's far enough removed from any wildlife that's bigger than I am.

After parking on the street, I go into Town Hall and follow the signs to the mayor's office. There's no one in the waiting room, so I call out, "Ashlyn, are you there?"

"Coming!" I hear in the distance. Moments later, she walks out of the back room. "Hello, boyfriend," she greets. She's got the cutest little smirk on her face.

"How's my girlfriend today?" I ask. Ashlyn looks positively stunning in her silky burgundy shirt and form-fitting slacks.

"Frazzled." She puts a finger in front of her lips before adding, "I'll tell you in the car."

We pass a woman in the hallway as we head toward the elevator. To help Ashlyn keep up her ruse, I loudly announce, "That was so nice of the mayor to meet with me."

Her mouth quirks into a faint smile. "My dad is nothing if not happy to talk to the citizens of Maple Falls." Once we're in the elevator and the doors close, she starts to laugh. "I almost missed my cue and asked you what you were talking about when you said you'd just met with my dad."

Shrugging, I tell her, "Just doing my part."

Once we're in my car, I ask her, "So, what's going on?"

"I talked to Jeremy Hunt this morning."

"Alexander MacDonald's lawyer, right?"

"Yeah. I asked if Mr. MacDonald might be willing to let Maple Falls buy the property back from him."

"What did he say?"

"He said that out of a sense of familial devotion, Mr. MacDonald wants to connect to his ancestor's land in some way."

"So, that's a no to selling it to Maple Falls?" I ask nervously. Now that I'm settled here, I really don't want to have to move to another town before the season starts. And if I don't move, that would mean a commute. I'm no longer sure I should bother looking at houses.

Ashlyn shakes her head. "He wouldn't come right out and say either way."

"So, all we can do is try to raise the money and hope for the best."

"But without an assurance that it will be accepted." She does not sound encouraged.

Trying to soothe her nerves, I tell her, "The guy didn't even know he was related to one of your town's founders until recently. How much *family devotion* could he possibly feel?" Instead of waiting for her to answer, I add, "I have a suspicion the almighty dollar is what he's really after."

She exhales loudly. "I don't know. I looked the guy up on the internet and he's already got mad stacks of cash. He certainly doesn't need our money."

"Don't give up," I tell her while I pull out on the street and follow the directions the realtor gave me to the first property. It's on a street called Maple Trail. As I search for the house number, I tell Ashlyn, "There are a lot of streets with the name Maple in them."

She snorts before itemizing, "There's Maple Farm Road, Maple Falls Road, Maple Harvest Lane, Maple Leaf Drive, and Maple Orchard Place …"

"It's like the town's whole identity is built around the maple tree."

"It could be worse. We could live in a town full of Buddha Belly bamboo trees."

"Never heard of them," I tell her.

"They're native to China but you see them in Southern California and Florida, as well. Can you imagine buying a house on Buddha Belly Bamboo Boulevard?"

"Uh, no." I tell her, "When I was on vacation in Hawaii, I learned about the Wiliwili tree. I could probably buy a house there on Wiliwili Way."

"Ever heard of the screaming trees?" she wants to know.

"Are you making fun of me?" I ask as I pull over to a white house with a for sale sign out front.

Shaking her head, she explains, "They get their names because every seventeen years the cicadas take up residence in them. The insects make such an obnoxious sound their temporary homes get dubbed the screaming trees." Without missing a beat, she adds, "But I could see how you might feel comfortable among them."

"Nice," I tell her before getting out of the car. I hurry around and open the passenger door for her and then offer her a hand.

A woman in her forties approaches us. She's wearing a business suit with tennis shoes. "Abigail Farmer," she announces. "Are you Jamie Hayes?"

"I am," I tell her while offering my other hand for her to shake. "This is my … er …" Shoot, I forgot to ask Ashlyn if it was okay to pretend we're a couple with everyone in town.

Ashlyn comes to my rescue by announcing, "I'm Ashlyn Thompkins."

"The mayor's daughter!" Abigail gushes excitedly. "I read the paper. What in the world are we going to do?"

Ashlyn removes her hand from mine before responding, "We're going to raise money and buy the land back."

Abigail tells us, "We had a big meeting this morning at the office and made the decision to only represent houses that aren't on Victor MacDonald's land. Can you imagine how this is going to affect the real estate market?" She turns and walks up the path to the front door.

Ashlyn leans into me and whispers, "I knew how serious this was, but what in the world are people going to do who own homes on Victor's land?"

Abigail opens the door. "You have three bedrooms and three bathrooms here. There's a fully finished basement, and a hot tub on the back deck. Why don't I let you two walk around and get a feel for the place?"

"Thank you, Abigail," I tell her.

As soon as we're out of her earshot, Ashlyn says, "You can't live here."

"Why?" I tease, "did you kiss someone here, too?"

She scrunches up her lips. "Ha, ha. No, I didn't kiss anyone here. Look out the window." She points to the woods behind the house.

"You think the bears would come out of there?"

She shrugs her shoulders. "They might, but that's not what I'm worried about." Before I can ask, she explains, "That's another preserve, and I think it's part of Victor's land."

"But the house isn't. Abigail said they weren't showing houses that could be affected by this."

"Yes, but if Alexander MacDonald won't let us buy the land from him, then he can do whatever he wants with that property. He might even build a giant grocery store there."

"I'm from New York City," I tell her. "Not only am I used to having businesses in my neighborhood, but I might consider a grocery store right outside my door a desirable thing."

"Until it brings down the cost of housing and you discover you've paid a lot more for your house than it will be worth." She's got a point.

The next house we look at is a possibility. But when Abigail asks if I want to place an offer on either of the homes, I tell her, "I'd better wait and find out what's in store for the Ice Breakers. If we can't use the arena in Maple Falls, we'll probably have to move the team."

Turning to Ashlyn, Abigail says, "I hope your dad knows what he's doing and can make this problem go away. If not, Maple Falls will be ruined."

The color drains from Ashlyn's face as she responds, "I hope he knows what he's doing too."

CHAPTER 23
ASHLYN

I'VE NEVER REALIZED how quickly time flies when you're in the middle of a crisis. That's probably because I've never been part of anything like what's happening to my hometown.

In the week since we found out about Alexander MacDonald, several local organizations have stepped up to the plate to offer help. The grade school is having a carwash this weekend and next. The high school is giving extra credit to students who do odd jobs around town and donate the money to our cause. The senior center is hosting a craft sale, and the Chamber of Commerce has placed donation cans in every local store. And from what I'm hearing, that's just the beginning.

Every day, I'm more and more convinced that we will raise the money. The only concern that remains is whether Alexander MacDonald will take it.

Even with everything on my plate, I've still managed to spend quite a lot of time with Jamie. It's not even like we've always made formal plans, either. One day we ran into each other at Shirley May's. After eating lunch together, I gave him the tour of the town I promised when we got sidetracked at the farmers' market. Another day, he came over to my parents' house and we watched a movie and ordered a pizza.

It's like we know our time is limited and we both want to see each other. Jamie is so easy to be with and on more than one occasion I've wished we were really dating. Barring that, I've started to think of him as a good friend.

Another high point in my life has been not having Phillip in the office. He still texts my dad all day, every day, and has even offered advice for how he can recover from his "flu"—some recipe involving horseradish, garlic, and fresh ginger. So gross.

I've managed to keep my dad's assistant occupied with busy work, but I can tell he's itching to have a real conversation with the mayor. Luckily for me, my parents are due home tonight.

I don't relish telling my dad what's happened, but I also feel confident I haven't dropped the ball in his absence. I'm currently working on the official purchase proposal that I've been instructed to send to Alexander MacDonald's business manager. It's a pretty impressive piece, if I do say so myself.

The desktop phone in my dad's office rings, momentarily sidetracking me. But it does this all day, so it's nothing new. "Mayor Thompkins' office, this is Ashlyn."

"Darling, it's your mother." I haven't talked to my mom for several days, so I'm surprised she's bothering to call me now when she's going to see me late tonight.

"Hey, Mom." I look at the clock and ask, "Are you already in Florida transferring planes?"

She responds with a question of her own. "Haven't you seen the news?"

"No," I tell her. "I'm a little bit busy trying to save Maple Falls. What's up?"

"Hurricane Bartholomew changed direction and it's headed right toward Barbados. They canceled our flight right before we boarded." She sounds scared which in turn makes me nervous.

"What are you going to do?"

"We came back to the resort. They're putting us up in the main building. They aren't sure the bungalows will make it." The quiver in my mom's voice catches me off guard. If she's worried, then they're in real trouble. Before I can console her, she adds, "It's a category five storm now and they don't know if it will slow down before it makes landfall."

I turn toward the computer and start typing. The first article that comes up paints a very bleak picture.

> Hurricane Bartholomew is on a collision course with Barbados. The airport has been closed, and locals have been advised to board up. Store shelves are emptying quickly. Residents close to the shoreline have already evacuated to disaster shelters where the Red Cross has begun setting up.

"Will the resort be able to feed you?" Worry fills my chest and starts to feel like a car is laying on top of it.

"I hope so, but your dad and I bought a bunch of stuff at the gift shop in the airport. Buying granola bars for five dollars a pop nearly killed him, let me tell you."

Even though my dad has always made decent money, he grew up poor. As such, he's notoriously frugal. He doesn't see the point in wasting money on things like name brand toilet paper and designer shoes. It's no wonder I love my job designing closets so much for people who buy whatever they want without caring how much anything costs.

"When is the hurricane supposed to make landfall?" I ask my mom.

She's quiet for a moment before answering, "At about midnight our time. You should watch the news to find out what happens. They tell us we may be without phone signals for a good while."

Real panic sets in and I start to sweat like an uncapped fire hydrant. "How long is a good while?"

"It could be days or weeks even. No one can know until the damage is assessed."

"Weeks?" This is bad on so many levels. The most serious being my parents' safety. I sent them to Barbados, which I suddenly realize is why I got such a great rate at the resort. I never bothered to check the weather forecast.

Then there's my dad not coming home to take over saving Maple Falls, which means that I have to stay. The least important in the grand scheme of things, but still rather significant to me, is that I have two jobs lined up for when I get back to LA. If I can't go back, I'll have to cancel them. Not only will that make a dent in my bank account, but it won't do wonders for my reputation.

"Can I talk to Dad?" I ask my mom.

She hands off the phone and the next voice I hear says, "It looks like your mom and I are in a bit of a pickle, huh?"

"Hi, Dad."

"How's everything going down at Town Hall?" he asks. "Is anyone missing me yet?"

I don't want him worrying about Maple Falls on top of facing the real danger that's coming his way, so I tell him, "Everything is great. Don't you worry."

"As much as I hate to admit this," he says, "I've really enjoyed this break. Thank you for coming home and lending a hand."

"Any idea how long you'll need me here?" I know he can't answer this with any authority, but I'm still hoping he lies and tells me only a few more days.

Instead of offering the lifeline I'm looking for, he answers, "Could be weeks. It's hard to say."

"If it's weeks," I tell him, "I'm going to have to let people know you're not here."

"Don't say anything until we know for sure. No sense upsetting folks." If he only knew how upset they already are, and why.

"Dad, I asked Mom to get you to record a few things that I might be able to use if I need to fool someone into thinking you're in the office. Did she ever tell you that?"

"She said something, but we got a little sidetracked." He's

clearly talking to my mom when he adds, "Isn't that right, dear?"

First of all, yay. I'm glad my parents are getting along, and their marriage is seemingly back on track, but also, *ew*. That is not an innuendo any kid wants to hear regarding their parents' relationship.

"When we hang up," I tell him, "call back and leave the following on my voicemail." I recite several lines that might come in handy.

My dad seems to take them all in stride except for the last one. "You can't really want me to say that. What could you possibly need that for?"

"It's just a little prank, Dad. Don't worry about it."

"My telling Phillip he's fired is a prank? That seems mean-spirited."

"Not at all." Lying through my teeth, I tell him, "We're actually getting along great. We tease each other all the time."

Our connection goes fuzzy for a moment. When it clears again, my dad says, "I'd better call you back and leave that voicemail now. I don't know how much longer we'll be able to call out." He pauses a beat before adding, "I love you, honey."

"I love you, too, Dad." Tears fill my eyes and for the first time, I worry that real harm might come to my parents.

In the background, my mom shouts, "I love you!" Then the line goes dead. I sit at my dad's desk for several minutes hoping they'll call back, but they don't.

There's only one person I want to talk to right now. Without stopping to consider why, I call him.

"You realize that we talk on the phone more than any other people our age, don't you?"

"Jamie …" I can't seem to say anything else. Instead, I burst into tears.

"Ashlyn, what's wrong?" His concern is immediate.

"It's my … they're in … it's so bad."

He takes my stilted communication to mean that I need help. "Where are you?"

"Town Hall," I tell him.

"I'm on my way," he says. "Should I call an ambulance? The police?"

I love how ready he is to jump into action. It comforts me enough to gain composure and tell him, "It's not me. It's my parents. Hurricane Bartholomew is heading right for them. Their flight got canceled and they have to ride it out."

"Oh, Ashlyn." His voice is warm and soothing. "I'm sorry. How about if I come over to your house and we can watch the news together? I can pick up fish and chips from Shirley May's."

Looking at the clock, I see that it's nearly six. Where in the world did the day go? "That would be great, thank you. I'm at the office, but I'll be home in twenty minutes or so."

"Are you okay to drive?" he asks. "Maybe I should pick you up."

"I'll be fine," I tell him. "Thank you, Jamie. I don't know what I'd do without you."

I'm surprised to realize that's the truth. Jamie Hayes is the most unexpected person to come into my life, but I can't imagine how I'd face any of this without him. I'd better watch myself, because even though I'll be in Maple Falls for longer than expected, I'm still not going to move here, so nothing more than friendship can happen between us.

CHAPTER 24
JAMIE

I CALL in a comfort food order to Shirley May's before leaving my cabin. Then I grab one of the several boxes of cereal I bought for the bear family sharing my yard. Walking out the door, I make eye contact with the papa bear. Then I throw the box behind him and make a run for it. I've gotten pretty good at this in the last week, all the while counting down the days until this crew goes into hibernation.

My phone rings once I get into my car and Bluetooth picks it up. Over the speakers I hear a voice I have not heard in a long enough time. "Jamie."

"Allegra?"

"Yes, it's me," she says. The sound of her is both familiar and oddly unsettling.

I don't feel like small talk, so I get right to the point. "Why are you calling?"

"I've been thinking about you a lot. I wanted to make sure you were okay."

The dormant anger in me starts to rise like a volcano coming to life. "Why do you suddenly care how I'm doing?"

She makes a low humming sound in her throat which is something she does when she doesn't quite know what to say. "I

… well … three years was a long time to be together. I guess I feel like we ended things a bit abruptly."

Putting the car into drive, I exit the property and pull out onto the main road. "I didn't end things," I tell her. "You did." There doesn't seem to be any reason to bring up the fact that I proposed twice, and both times she told me she wasn't ready.

"It was my fault, Jamie, and I'm sorry."

I might have appreciated this conversation months ago, but it's not doing much for me right now. "Is that all you called to say?"

"No. I wanted to let you know that Brett and I are taking a little break."

"Pardon me if this sounds rude, Allegra, but why do you think I care?"

She inhales deeply before telling me, "I left without giving us a fair chance, Jamie. I should have told you how I was feeling."

As I drive toward town, I realize the trees are changing color more every day and an unexpected peace washes over me. "There's nothing you can do about it now."

"Can we talk in person?" she asks. Her voice sounds pained, like a wounded animal.

"To what end?" I ask. I mean, I left New York for Washington because of her. I hardly want to see her now.

"I need to see you. I need to talk to you. I need closure." She sure does have a lot of needs for someone who caused this situation.

"You left me high and dry," I tell her.

"I know."

"I don't owe you anything, Allegra."

"No, you don't. But we were once very much in love and even if you hate me now, please try to remember the woman I used to be to you. Meet me for her sake."

Turning onto Main Street, I park in front of Shirley May's. "The woman I used to love doesn't exist anymore, Allegra. I'm sorry you're having a hard time, but I'm not the person to share your troubles with."

Her soft sob stirs a tiny speck of sympathy in me. I did love Allegra, and as I recently told Ashlyn, part of me always will. But even so, I can't put myself through any more. I'm finally coming out of my grief and getting on with my life. There's no point in moving backwards.

"I'm sorry I called," Allegra eventually says. "I'm sorry for everything. I really made a mess of things."

I don't try to console her. She did make a mess of things, and I've paid a huge price for that. I abandoned my town and my team just to get away from the disaster she left in her wake. "If that's all …" I say.

"Jamie." Allegra's tone is pure begging now. "If you change your mind …"

"I won't," I tell her with finality.

"I still love you."

"Have a good life, Allegra." I disconnect the call. How dare she contact me and ask me to see her? She must think I'm a complete fool to put myself in a position where she could hurt me again.

Getting out of the car, I feel the cool evening breeze on my face. Taking a deep breath, I fancy I can smell the change in season. I've only been in Maple Falls a short time, and I'm still not sure I'm going to ever feel like it's my home, but right now I'm so glad to be here and not in New York, I could cheer.

Walking into the diner, Peggy calls out, "Jamie!" I love how I'm already on a first-name basis with both her and Shirley May.

"Hi, Peggy," I say. "I placed an order to go."

"Having supper with Ashlyn?"

One of the weirdest things to get used to is that there is zero privacy in this small town. "Why would you think that?" I ask.

"You got her favorite food," the waitress says. "Plus, I heard that you and Ashlyn are a number. Good for you. You couldn't find yourself a nicer gal."

"You're right," I tell her. An image of Allegra pops into my mind and I realize that Ashlyn is so much better for me. It's too bad she's going back to LA and won't ever be more than a friend. Yet, now that the press has picked up on our fake relationship, I need to play the part.

"Her parents will be happy to have her back in town," Peggy says.

"I'm not sure she's moving home."

Peggy gives me a slow wink. "Of course she'll move home. Long distance relationships are tough, and Ash is too smart for that kind of nonsense."

After paying for our food, Peggy hands a brown shopping bag across the counter. "I put in extra pie for my girl. It really is her favorite."

"That's very nice of you, Peggy. I'll make sure to make it up to you once the season starts. Maybe some rink-side tickets?"

"Oh, honey, that's sweet, but I don't like hockey." She thinks for a beat before saying, "But if you get any basketball tickets, you let me know."

It's strange for a professional athlete to have someone be so nice to them when they're not looking for some kind of payback. Long ago, I learned it was par for the course that people sucked up in hopes of a better favor being returned.

And even though I've only been in town for a short time, that has not been my experience with people here. They are genuinely nice to you because that's just who they are.

Getting back into the car, I drive three minutes to Ashlyn's parents' house. I glance around the neighborhood before turning into her driveway. That's when I see an older lady in the house across the street staring out her window right at me. I think about waving in greeting, but as we make eye contact, she lets the curtain sheers close in front of her. The shadow of her remains so I know she's still watching.

I grab our dinner before getting out of the car and walking up to the front door. Ashlyn answers it before I can knock. "I was watching out the window," she tells me by way of greeting.

"You're not the only one." I take a step back and point across the street.

Ashlyn huffs, "That's our neighbor, Mary-Ellen McCluskey. She's the biggest gossip in town. Within an hour, she will have called everyone she knows and told them that you're here." Suddenly Ashlyn's face morphs into a smile. Stepping out of the house, she waves her hands and calls out, "Hi, Mrs. McCluskey!" A face appears in the window. Ashlyn gestures toward me. "This is Jamie Hayes. He has a meeting with my dad!"

The drapes on the window across the street fall back into place before the front door opens. "What was that, dear? I couldn't hear you."

"I said this is Jamie Hayes. He's the captain of the Ice Breakers. He's meeting my dad."

I lean in toward Ashlyn and whisper, "This is a weird way to introduce me."

She quietly responds, "Trust me, it's the best way of dealing with a gossip. She's less interested in the way she's meeting you than in the fact that she's getting details for the story she's about to spread around town."

Mrs. McCluskey calls back, "I hear that you and this man are dating. Is that true?"

"We're friends," Ashlyn tells her, neither confirming nor denying.

"I see." Ashlyn's neighbor excitedly adds, "Well, I'd better get going. I have supper in the oven."

Ashlyn waves again before pulling me inside. "*Supper* is code for a million people to call."

"How are you doing?" I ask her as she leads the way into the kitchen.

She pulls down plates from the cabinet before retrieving silverware from the drawer. "I'm scared. I can't believe I sent my parents on a trip in the middle of a hurricane zone during hurricane season. Who does that?"

Sitting down at the kitchen table, I remind her, "You needed to find something last minute."

"And now we know why it was available." She pours two glasses of water from the pitcher in the refrigerator and brings them over to the table while I take our food out of the bag. This whole scene is so domestic it makes me yearn for more.

A sudden tension fills the air around us like there's a third person in the room. "Ashlyn …" I start to say.

She doesn't let me finish my thought. "Thanks for bringing supper over."

Sitting down across the table from me, she opens her food container. It seems like she's trying really hard not to look at me.

I suppose now is not the time to tell her how I'm starting to feel. She clearly doesn't want to hear it or she would have let me finish speaking. Trying to regain the easiness of companionship we were enjoying, I tell her, "I just had an interesting call."

CHAPTER 25
ASHLYN

HAVING dinner with Jamie feels like the most natural thing in the world. His presence is comforting and highly disconcerting at the same time. I've obviously felt attraction for the men I've dated in the past, but I've never felt as drawn to them as I am to Jamie. Note to self, Ashlyn: *You are not dating Jamie Hayes. He is your friend.*

"So, tell me about this mysterious call," I say.

Opening his food container, Jamie transfers his fish and chips to the plate in front of him. "I just got off the phone with Allegra."

My fork stops halfway to my mouth. "Really? Did you call her, or did she call you?"

"She called me."

"Why?"

He tips his head from side to side before answering. "She said she's taking a break from the guy she left me for. She wants to see me."

Even though I think Allegra was an idiot to leave Jamie, I can fully understand how she could want him back. However, I'm not thrilled about it. "Wow. What are you going to do?"

"I'm obviously not going to see her," he says. "Why? Do you think I should?"

"I … um … well …" I absolutely *don't* think he should see her, but I'm also beginning to wonder if Jamie might be starting to have romantic feelings for me. *Just like I'm having for him.* Which is not good and the only reason I tell him, "I don't see how it could hurt anything."

He looks up at me with shock in his big blue eyes. "Why would I bother? I'm not a big enough idiot to consider taking her back. You don't think I should take her back, do you?"

I put my first bite of fish into my mouth and chew it slowly before swallowing. Then I take a sip of water. "You told me yourself there's a part of you that will always love Allegra."

"Yeah, but that doesn't mean I can forgive her." He looks appalled at the very notion.

"Love is weird," I tell him. "Take my parents. My mom felt like my dad never made her a priority and because of that she was going to leave him. Even though Allegra left you for a billionaire, you even admitted that you didn't make enough time for your relationship with her. If that's true, it's easy to see that she didn't feel like a priority …" I let the rest of the thought dangle in the air.

"I did say that, but I still have a shred of self-respect left. And unlike your parents, Allegra and I were never married."

I'm actually happy he doesn't want to see her, but that doesn't mean we can let anything more develop between us. Even though my stay here has been extended, I am still going to leave Maple Falls. "I should introduce you to my neighbor, Clara," I tell him.

He looks confused. "Why?"

"She's a lovely single mother of two." After a beat, I add, "She's doing the social media for the Ice Breakers."

"I thought I made it clear that I wasn't looking." He sounds mad.

"But if you're truly not interested in getting back together with Allegra, then why not date a nice woman who lives right in the same town that you do?"

He cocks an eyebrow and his gaze turns intense. "I'm dating *you*. At least according to the press. How would it look if I started two-timing you with someone else?"

I hadn't thought about that. "I could introduce you now, and then after I go home, you could ask Clara out." Even as I say this, I feel raw jealousy explode in my gut. I don't want Jamie to date Clara. I don't want him to date anyone.

Jamie pushes back from the table. His forearms flex as he crosses his arms across his hockey shirt. "I've already met Clara."

"Really?"

"As you mentioned, she's doing social media for the Ice Breakers, and I'm the captain of that team."

"Oh, yeah." I giggle nervously. "That makes sense." Then I ask, "She's nice, right?"

He shrugs. "I guess. But she certainly isn't giving off single vibes. I think she might already have someone."

"Oh." We still haven't gotten together so I don't know her story.

"As far as the world is concerned," he reminds me, "I'm dating you. And now that you're going to be staying in Maple Falls for a longer time, I would like to ask you to please be my plus one at the Ice Breakers Inaugural Ball."

The thought of going to a ball with Jamie makes my skin tingle with possibility. "When is it?"

"Next week, on the fourteenth."

While I'm hoping my parents will be home by then, that doesn't seem realistic now that they're about to be caught in the middle of a hurricane. Even so, I say, "What if I'm back in LA by then?"

"I suppose I could hire you to come home for the night and go to the ball with me."

"Hire me? That makes it sound like I'm some kind of escort."

I'm trying to sound offended but even so, I can't help but wonder what it would be like to dance in Jamie's arms.

"It's nothing seedy like that," he says. "Merely an offer to pay you for your time and travel. I would do the same for my sister if I asked her to be my plus-one."

I suddenly feel less flattered by the invitation. "You have a sister?" I ask. As much time as Jamie and I have spent together, I'm realizing I still don't know much about his personal life.

"I do. Her name is Jasmine."

Still smarting at the comparison with his sibling, I ask, "Then why don't you invite her?" I dig into my coleslaw while he thinks about it.

"Because I'm supposed to be dating you. And now that Allegra is single again, I don't want the press speculating about whether we'll get back together."

"Huh." I finish the bite in my mouth before telling him, "*If* I'm still here, I'll go with you."

"And if you've gone back to LA?"

"Then I'll be working and won't be able to take any more time off." The real reason is that if I've left Maple Falls, I don't see the wisdom in letting myself fall more for Jamie than I already have.

He reaches his hand across the table and gently takes my hand in his. He gives it a light shake. "You have yourself a deal."

After we finish eating, Jamie and I head into the family room. I turn the TV on and sit down on the opposite side of the couch from him.

The news broadcast starts out like they all do, predicting doom and gloom and terrible outcomes. I do my best to remember that hurricanes change course all the time. Yet even though I try to keep positive, the newscast gets more and more discouraging by the minute.

After an hour of this, the announcer says, "Hurricane Bartholomew has reached over four hundred miles across with wind speeds topping two hundred miles per hour. Folks, we have not seen a storm this size in over a decade. The last one that was even close was Hurricane Patricia in 2015. The only reason that one didn't cause more damage is because it hit an isolated part of Mexico. Conversely, Bartholomew is on a collision course for Barbados. The outcome could be catastrophic."

The anchor pauses as though trying to collect himself before adding, "If you're a person of faith, I think it would be fair to suggest you take a moment to offer a prayer for those poor people who are about to get the walloping of a lifetime."

My body collapses in on itself like I'm melting into the sofa. Jamie immediately scoots over until we're sitting with our sides pressed against each other. Then he puts his arm around me and holds me close. "They're going to be okay," he soothes.

For the briefest of moments, I don't think. I just snuggle into him and feel the heat emanate from his body. The sensation is pure heaven, so I let myself relish in his strength. Unfortunately, panic returns quickly.

"You don't know they're going to be okay," I tell him. "They might be hurt. But even if they make it through the storm, they have to survive for God knows how long and in what kind of conditions until help arrives."

"I don't think your parents' fate is to die in a hurricane. Especially when the whole reason they went away was to save their marriage."

I turn toward him so quickly, I nearly head butt him. "You believe in fate?"

"I don't *not* believe in it." He explains, "It's hard to think that everything happens by random chance."

"Do you think you coming to Maple Falls was your fate?"

He looks pensive before answering, "I don't know. All I know is that I would have never moved here had Allegra not left me. Not only that, but the hockey player I've loathed most in my career is on my team, and I learned that the reason I've disliked him was based on an inaccuracy."

"So, you think you were meant to come here?"

"I met you, didn't I? Making a new friend seems like something that might have been written in the stars." The twinkle in his eyes causes goosebumps to pop up all over my body.

As terrified as I am for my parents, Jamie is making me feel better. "I suppose that's possible," I tell him.

"Why would fate put me through a break-up, and reunite me with someone I've vowed to avoid only to harm my new friend's parents?"

"You make fate sound like it's an intelligent force."

He thinks for a moment before explaining, "We all have different beliefs, but I think that we get to choose the people who come into our lives before we come here. I don't think every action and outcome is known, but I think we give ourselves the opportunity to achieve the best result for ourselves."

Our conversation is taking a philosophical turn. I like knowing Jamie is a deep thinker, even though it surprises me at the same time. Not because I don't think he's smart, I just never think of professional athletes as ponderers of life. For clarification, I ask, "You think when we were still in heaven, you and I sat down and decided to be friends in this life?"

"Why not?" he asks.

"And you think our friendship is worth losing Allegra for?"

He exhales loudly before answering, "I think that maybe Allegra has chosen something different for herself."

"Maybe she's changing her mind," I offer. "If you thought enough of her to stay with her for three years, maybe she's worth fighting for." I probably shouldn't have said that out loud, because the more time I spend with Jamie, the more I find myself composing scenarios where we can be together.

"I guess it's possible." He doesn't sound like he believes it though.

"It's in line with your belief system," I tell him. "You think we bring people into our worlds by design but what happens between us when we get here is up in the air."

"I think," he says as he pulls me closer, "that we still have freedom of choice, but within the confines of some basic parameters. It's kind of like fate but without being cut and dry."

If that's so, then it's possible for something more to happen between me and Jamie. But it's also possible he'll get back with Allegra. Either way, I decide, "Maybe whatever happens to my parents is their fate and has nothing to do with me."

"Exactly," he says. "We're all our own people and we all have our own agendas. They just overlap throughout our journeys."

Resting my head against his shoulder, I tell him, "I sure hope my parents have a happy ending to their journey. This hurricane may not be my fault, but I don't think I could live with myself if something bad happened to them."

"Then let's decide nothing bad will happen to them. Let's send them all the positive energy we can."

"You mean pray?"

"Prayer, energy, call it whatever you want. No matter the name, it's all positive."

With my head still leaning on my new friend, I silently ask God to protect my parents and all the other people on the island. I ask Him to help Maple Falls stay the lovely town it's always been. As a final boon, I ask that He help guide me in my life so that I might find my own happy ending. If that ending includes Jamie Hayes, all the better.

CHAPTER 26
JAMIE

I CAN'T SEEM to get Ashlyn's parents out of my mind. The hurricane hit Barbados as a Class 5 storm and caused a historic amount of damage. Reports coming out of the island for the last week have been sporadic. As predicted, there has been no telephone service. The little news we've gotten has made it clear the damage is extensive enough that travel will not be possible for at least another week.

The upside, for me anyway, is that Ashlyn will be staying in Maple Falls. The downside, of course, is that she's very worried about her parents.

My thoughts have been jumping all over the place today and briefly shift to hockey. Preseason practice has ended and we're getting ready for our first game against the Great Lakes Vikings. The Ice Breakers are well on their way to being a finely honed team, and not just on the ice. We're working hard to help the town raise the money needed to buy their land back.

Last week at the farmers' market, I even got drawn into something called "Drenched for Defense." They essentially sold buckets of water that people got to throw at some of my teammates. While I didn't sign up for it, I still somehow got roped into it.

Ashlyn's neighbor, Clara, has been working on building our social media presence, which we're using to help promote the upcoming bachelor auction. Ashlyn and I continue to see a lot of each other. We mostly brainstorm ideas to help the town, but we still manage to find time to talk about ourselves. She's mentioned on more than one occasion that she feels I should talk to Allegra in person. I've maintained that when someone cheats on you, they lose all rights to your time. She claims that three years should buy you a final meeting. We've agreed to disagree.

I'm currently sitting at Shirley May's eating breakfast, thinking about the wild turn my life has taken in the last few months. I thought I had my whole future worked out. I was eventually going to marry Allegra, and then we would have had a family, and maybe a dog or some cats. We would buy a summer house in the Hamptons and the kids and I would travel with Allegra whenever she had a job. As much as I knew I would retire in a few years, I was just as certain that Allegra would not. Her identity largely revolves around her looks, and I assumed she would always need to be in the spotlight to be validated.

But now we're no longer a couple, and I've left New York. Not only that, but I'm playing with a new team, and I have a new woman in my life. Even though Ashlyn and I are not romantically involved, she means more to me every day.

I'm so lost in thought that I don't realize I have company until I hear someone demand, "What's going on with you and Ashlyn Thompkins?"

I look up to find the mayor's assistant looming over me. I don't bother to let him know that I recognize him from the emergency town hall meeting. Instead, I ask, "Who are you?"

"I'm Phillip Bane. I work for Mayor Thompkins."

"How is it any of your business what's going on between me and Ashlyn?"

"The mayor is worried about his daughter. She's going back to Los Angeles, you know."

"If the mayor is worried, why isn't the mayor the one talking to me?"

Phillip huffs loudly. "Mayor Thompkins is very busy trying to save Maple Falls. He's asked me to talk to you." Phillip sits down across the table from me.

"You've talked to the mayor, have you?" I ask. He's obviously lying because Ashlyn hasn't even been able to talk to her dad. I immediately feel the same loathing for this man that she does.

"I talk to him *all* the time," Phillip lies. "I'm his right hand."

I wipe a small amount of pancake syrup off my mouth before asking, "And the mayor has asked you to speak with me?"

"Not in as many words," Phillip says. "But I think you should know he isn't happy about what's happening between you and his daughter."

"I see." Stepping out of the booth, I stand up and tell him, "I suppose he should take that up with me directly then. I don't talk to lackeys."

"Lackeys?!" Phillip is offended, which was of course my intention. "I'll have you know that *I* am the next mayor of this town, and you should want to be on good terms with me."

"I didn't realize Mayor Thompkins was stepping down," I tell him.

"I'm running for office when his term is up." Phillip practically bounces to his feet like a fully wound jack-in-the-box. With his fists clenched at his sides, he appears to be contemplating getting physical.

"If I'm still in Maple Falls at that time," I tell him, "I'll be voting for your opponent."

"You'd better watch yourself, Mr. Hayes." As if this twerp could do anything to me.

Instead of continuing this ridiculous conversation, I simply drop a twenty on the table to cover my bill, and then I walk out of the restaurant. I'm about to fish my phone out of my pocket to fill Ashlyn in on what just took place when I run into the last person in the world I expected to see.

"Allegra, what are you doing here?" My chic ex is standing in front of me with a look of raw anticipation on her face.

"I told you that I wanted to talk to you, Jamie."

"I told you there was no reason," I respond.

"Yes, well, I'm here now." Allegra is wearing boots with a three-inch heel, so she stands nearly eye-to-eye with me. "All I want is a few minutes of your time."

"You flew across the country for a few minutes of my time?" I ask with astonishment. This is uncharacteristic behavior, as Allegra is the kind of person who lets the world come to her, not vice versa.

She steps closer to me and makes a move to take my hand. There is no way in heck I'm going to have a conversation with her publicly. The last thing I want is for anyone to see us together and start to speculate. Or, God forbid, take a picture and sell it to the tabloids.

"You can come to my cabin, and we can talk there," I tell her.

She looks so happy that I feel a spark of something start to bloom in my chest. It's not happiness, but perhaps an emotion related to sympathy.

"I'll drive with you," she says.

I motion toward my SUV and then unlock the doors with my remote. I don't bother to open her door for her like I always did when we were together. Instead, I walk around and get into the driver's side. Allegra stands on the sidewalk, seemingly expecting her door to magically pop open.

Turning on the car, I lower the passenger side window and tell her, "Get in."

She reluctantly opens the door for herself. Once she's sitting next to me, I pull out onto the street. We drive in silence for a minute or two, before she says, "I'm having a hard time seeing you living in a place like this."

"Yeah, well, this is my new life." I feel the need to add, "Thanks to you."

She shrinks slightly in my peripheral vision. "I'm sorry, Jamie. I'm sorry for what I did to you. It wasn't right and it wasn't fair."

"You are correct," I tell her.

"I wasn't thinking clearly," she says. "I made a mistake."

I slow the car down and turn into my driveway. I don't turn off the car once I park. Instead, I tell her, "If that's all you needed to say, I'll take you back into town."

"That's not all I came here for." Before I can warn her about the bear family, she steps out of the car and starts cat-walking toward the cabin. That's when she comes face to face with mama bear.

Allegra releases a bloodcurdling scream so loud I'm surprised it doesn't shatter our eardrums. In response, the mama bear merely turns and ambles toward the closest tree. That's when the baby bear shoots across the path toward his mother. Allegra shrieks again before turning around and running toward me. "There are bears here!" she shouts.

I take her hand and pull her toward my front porch. I've gotten better at dealing with my neighbors in the last several days, but even so, I don't dilly dally. Once we're inside, I drop Allegra's hand. Going into the kitchen, I ask her, "Do you want some water?"

"Yes, please." She follows me and sits down at the small kitchen table. "What are you doing living in the woods with bears?"

"I didn't know they lived here when I moved in," I tell her.

"Jamie." Her tone is full of pleading. I put her glass of water in front of her, and after she takes a sip, she says. "Please move back home."

"Why would I do that?" I ask, sitting across from her. "I play for the Ice Breakers now."

"The Blades would take you back in a heartbeat."

"I'm the captain of a new team, Allegra. I have a contract." I feel the need to add, "There's nothing left for me in New York."

I can tell I've hurt her, and even though she also hurt me, I still feel bad about it.

Before I get a chance to soften my words, she proceeds with, "Brett and I have broken up for good," like I'm supposed to somehow know what this has to do with me. I don't have to wait long for clarification. "I want us to try again, Jamie. We were together for a long time. We meant a lot to each other."

"Until you left me for another man," I remind her.

"I'm very sorry about that. I was wrong."

I can't help but wonder why Allegra thinks I'll just forgive her and go back. "You made a fool out of me in front of the whole world."

"I'll tell the press how wrong I was. I'll tell them anything you want me to."

I look at my ex like I'm seeing her for the first time. While stunningly beautiful, with her sleek, long brown hair and matching eyes, there's something completely unrecognizable about her. I feel like I never really knew her.

"There's nothing to tell the press, Allegra. I don't want you back. I've moved on."

Her eyes narrow slightly before she says, "I've heard. With some small-town girl named Ashlyn." She says Ashlyn's name like it's a curse word.

"Yes," I lie. "I've moved on with Ashlyn."

"You haven't been with her for that long, Jamie. She can't mean much to you."

"What does time have to do with anything, Allegra? You and I were together for three years, and yet you had no problem dumping me for a man you'd just met."

"And I'm sorry about that!" She jumps to her feet and starts a righteous pace across my kitchen floor. "Brett isn't the man I thought he was."

"I don't know who you thought he was," I tell her, "but even

I knew he was a three-time married lothario with quite a track record for breaking hearts."

She stops pacing and comes back to the table. Dropping to her knees in front of me, she puts her hands on top of mine. "I was confused. I was sad that we didn't spend a lot of time together. I was vulnerable."

I gently remove my hands from under hers. "I'm sorry you were unhappy. I truly am. But you made your choice. We had a long run, but our time together is over. I'm with Ashlyn now." Even though I intellectually know there's no truth to what I'm saying, my heart still wants to believe it.

"You can't love her!" Allegra declares heatedly.

"Why is that?"

She seems to finally realize she can't use time against me. "Because I still love you!"

"I don't know how many times you have to hear this, Allegra, but I have stopped loving you. You are my past, not my future."

I have never felt comfortable watching someone cry, so I'm unprepared for the coldness I feel when my ex bursts into tears. "I made a mistake," she wails. "I want to make things right."

"What's done is done," I tell her. "You and I are no more."

Allegra stands up slowly with a rigidity in her shoulders that makes it clear she's finally hearing my words. "You can take me back into town now."

As she walks to the front door, I wonder why we needed to have this out in person. Standing up, I grab my keys along with a box of granola and join her. Stepping out on the porch before her, I throw the cereal into the woods and say, "That will only buy us a couple of minutes. Let's go."

Once we're back in the car, Allegra asks, "How can you live in a place like this? It's so rural. So barbaric."

"Bears are part of nature. They were here before us." When did I start defending the bear population? Just a couple of weeks ago, I thought just like Allegra did, but now I'm taking their side against her. I must be adapting faster than I realized.

We make the trip into town in silence. Once we arrive back at Shirley May's, I pull into a parking spot and tell Allegra, "Have a safe trip home."

"That's it? You don't have anything else to say to me?" Tears start to pool in her doe-like eyes again.

"I don't know what else you want me to say. I'm sorry about the way things ended between us, but I wasn't the one who ended us. I'm sorry you're having regrets, but there's nothing I can do for you."

"You could give me another chance." She says this so quietly I wonder if I imagined it.

"I have a meeting at the arena," I lie. "I need to go."

She finally takes the hint and gets out of my car. Before shutting the door behind her, she says, "I love you, Jamie. I really do." When I don't respond in kind, she closes the door.

Two weeks ago, before I met Ashlyn, I might have considered going back to Allegra. But not now. Now I know there's something better out there for me. I just have to try to convince Ashlyn to give me a chance to prove that I'm the one for her.

CHAPTER 27
ASHLYN

SEVEN DAYS later and I still don't have an official update on my parents. I'd like to think this is good news because if they were somehow injured or worse, I would think I would have been notified by somebody. It's still agony waiting to hear, and of course my imagination has been triggered into overdrive. Like what if everyone is dead and no one can make calls?

I don't really have a ton of time to speculate, however, because Maple Falls is up in arms and oddly divided about how they feel regarding Alexander MacDonald taking over his ancestor's land. The store owners and people directly affected are panic stricken and want the town to buy the land back. Then there are those who want the land developed so Maple Falls can "join the twenty-first century" and get a warehouse club so they can buy rotisserie chickens.

The topic of preservation vs. progress is a bigger one than I ever thought it would be. I just assumed everyone wanted life to stay the same. Apparently, the lure of new jobs and bulk toilet paper is real.

All I know is that I'm currently sitting in the middle of a heated town council meeting and all I want to do is run out the door and not stop until I get to the airport. But if I left town then

I wouldn't see Jamie anymore and he's become a big part of my life. I keep reminding myself that I don't live here, so Jamie is nothing more than a nice distraction. The problem is that I'm really bad about listening to my own advice.

Jeremy Hunt, Alexander MacDonald's lawyer, has shown up in town and is currently blathering on about how important it is for Maple Falls to have the kind of infrastructure needed for a town that has its own NHL team. He's so superior sounding it's all I can do not to stand up and throw a shoe at him.

Before I can act out this fantasy, Phillip sits down next to me and hisses in my ear, "Your dad can't still be sick. What's really going on, Ashlyn?"

I give him my most scathing side-eye. "The latest word is viral gastroenteritis with a side of lactose intolerance." I've Googled just about everything possible and this is the most believable, non-life-threatening, diagnosis I could come up with.

"Your dad is not lactose intolerant," Phillip says like he's suddenly a medical expert. "He has milk in his coffee, and he eats cheese and ice cream."

I respond with a death glare. "People can develop allergies at any time, you moron."

Phillip smacks his palm against the tabletop, making a loud enough sound that a few people turn in our direction. In a quieter voice, he declares, "I want to talk to him, and I want to talk to him soon."

"I assure you, he's not feeling up to a real conversation," I retort. "Plus, he says he's been texting you."

Phillip's eyes narrow slowly. "He talks to you and your mother. Come to think of it, I haven't seen your mom around town either."

"That's because she's been home taking care of my dad, Phillip."

My mom had been handling her end of things beautifully from Barbados, but now that she doesn't have phone reception, people have started to call me to see where she is. This whole thing is getting more and more complicated.

I wish I could just tell everybody where my parents are, but now that we're three weeks into this thing, if they knew dad didn't come home when he found out what was going on, it would certainly affect their opinion of him. Especially because my dad does not want the town to know my mom was going to leave him.

Picking up my phone, I pretend to get a text. As soon as there's a break in conversation, I raise my hand and tell the gathering, "I'm so sorry but I need to take this incoming call. I've been looking into a few things, and this might be the information I've been waiting for." Then I practically run out of the room.

Phillip, of course, follows. Pointing to the phone in my hand, he accuses, "You aren't taking a call."

"They're calling in five minutes," I snarl back.

"Who's calling?"

I ignore him and walk toward the ladies' room at the end of the hall. My dad's pesky assistant trails behind, but luckily he has the sense to let me go in by myself. Locking myself into a stall, I take out my dad's phone and text Phillip.

MAYOR THOMPKINS

> Phillip, I need you to take detailed notes of the town hall meeting and email them to me after it's over.

PHILLIP

Sir, are you feeling any better?

MAYOR THOMPKINS

> This is the sickest I've ever been. Alicia is going to take me into Spokane to see a specialist this week. I'll keep you updated.

PHILLIP

I've been out of the office for a week, but I'd better head back in. I'm sure the cleaning crew has killed any germs by now.

The last thing I want is for Phillip to come back to work, so I hurry to come up with a reason he shouldn't. Unfortunately, the only thing that comes to mind is a real stretch.

> MAYOR THOMPKINS
>
> Good idea. I need you to call an exterminator in the morning and have him check into the snake situation. Several people have reported that the grounds are infested with garter snakes.

PHILLIP

Snakes?!

> MAYOR THOMPKINS
>
> They aren't poisonous, so there's nothing to worry about. But I understand they even found one in the men's room.

PHILLIP

I can't. I mean, I can't …

> MAYOR THOMPKINS
>
> What can't you do?

But there's no response. I peek out of the bathroom and see Phillip standing so still it's like he's playing that old childhood game, statue maker. His pallor is even a grey-like marble.

I take a tentative step toward him, and say, "Phillip, are you okay?"

He shakes his head slowly. "I … I … How can I leave the building knowing there are snakes out there?"

Shoot, I didn't think about that. I wrack my brain to come up with something to get him out of the building. "The snakes only come out during the day," I tell him. "They sleep at night."

"But … but … they're out there."

"They're asleep, Phillip. They can't hurt you." Darn if I don't feel a little bit of sympathy for the guy. I reach out and take his arm and offer, "I'll walk you out to your car. I'll even go first."

His head bobs up and down slowly, but he looks like he's in

some kind of fear-induced trance. As soon as we exit the building, Phillip pulls his arm away from me and practically sprints down the walkway toward the parking garage. I follow after him at a more dignified pace.

As soon as he gets to his car, he says, "I'm sorry, but I won't be able to come into the office until the snake problem is taken care of. I don't like snakes." Then he pulls out like the hounds of hell are chasing him with intent.

Even though I feel bad playing Phillip's worst fear against him, I'd be lying if I didn't say inventing a snake infestation was genius on my part. After all, desperate times call for desperate measures. And I am nothing if not totally desperate to get that man to stop asking questions about my parents.

Before I can go back inside, my phone rings. Looking down at the screen, I almost fall over in shock. "Mom! How are you? I've been a nervous wreck worrying about you guys."

"Wow, honey, what a rush!" She sounds oddly excited.

"The hurricane was a rush? Were you terrified? Are you both okay?"

"It was amazing!" She sounds like a ten-year-old who just took her first ride on an adult rollercoaster. "We're both good, but the island is a disaster. I'm not sure when we're going to be able to get out of here."

"I'm just glad you're okay," I tell her, suddenly feeling like the weight of the world is off my shoulders.

"How are things in Maple Falls?"

"Same as they were a week ago, except now some blowhard who works for Alexander MacDonald has shown up in town. He's trying to get everyone on board with the idea of developing the land."

"It sounds like they won't take the money even if you can raise it."

"I'm not giving up on that yet, Mom. We're going full steam ahead to come up with the cash. Then, if need be, I'll appeal to the man in person. According to his lawyer he's out of the country, but I'll fly to Bangladesh and plead with him if I have to."

"And if he doesn't take it? What does that mean for businesses already on the land?"

"I don't know," I tell her. "But now that you and dad are safe, I'll be spending all of my time trying to figure that out."

"Good girl," my mom says. "Your dad and I love you so much, dear. There isn't anything you can't do once you set your mind to it."

"Thanks, Mom. That means the world."

I'm so relieved my parents are okay that as soon as we hang up, all I want to do is celebrate. So instead of going back into the meeting I call the only person I want to share this news with.

"Ashlyn, hey. What's up?" Jamie asks.

"Want to take me out for a glass of champagne?"

"Did you get Alexander MacDonald to agree to sell the land?"

"Nope. But I heard from my parents," I tell him. "They're okay."

"That's the best news ever!" He sounds like he means it too. "How about if I stop by the store and buy a bottle and we can drink it at my place?"

"Your place?"

"Not as a date," he says. "Just a place where we won't be a source of interest."

I no longer care if it's a date or not. In fact, if given a choice, I think I'd like to go out on a real date with Jamie. I'm just not prepared to tell him that quite yet.

CHAPTER 28
JAMIE

AFTER HANGING UP WITH ASHLYN, I hurry into town and buy a bottle of champagne, along with some cheese, crackers, and a couple more boxes of granola. *Hibernation cannot come soon enough.*

By the time I get home, Ashlyn's already standing on my porch. "I beat you here," she calls out.

"You should have waited in your car. It would have been safer." That's when I notice all the empty cereal boxes in her arms. She must have gone into the woods to pick them up.

"Have you been feeding the bears?" she asks accusingly.

"Maybe, a little."

"Jamie," she says sternly. "That's not a good idea. You really don't want to become too familiar with them."

"Nor do I want to become their dinner." Before she can tell me that bears don't eat people, I add, "Or a toy they rip apart for kicks."

I hurry to open the front door, relieved that the bear family is off somewhere else. I step back so Ashlyn can go in first and then I follow her. "So, tell me about your parents."

She walks into the living area and sits down on the overstuffed sofa. "There's not much to say other than they're okay.

They don't know when they'll be able to leave, but they have enough food and water."

I walk into the kitchen and take two glasses out of the cabinet. Then I pull the bottle of already-chilled champagne out of the bag and open it. Once our drinks are poured, I carry the glasses into the living room. After handing one to Ashlyn, I raise mine in the air, and toast, "To your parents' safe return."

She clinks her glass against mine before taking a sip. Then she says, "You were the first person I wanted to tell when I heard the news."

"That would be a compliment if I wasn't the only person you could tell."

Her cheeks flush slightly. "I could have told Marcy."

"Ah, yes, I forgot about the town's accountant." I wink and add, "Then I'm extremely flattered that between the two of us, you wanted to tell me first."

After taking another sip of her drink, she says, "You've been so supportive and encouraging. I've really appreciated that."

I sit down next to her. "It's been my pleasure. After all, I can't have my girlfriend eaten up by anxiety."

She rolls her eyes. "Then you should write me a check for two and a half million so I can get Alexander MacDonald off our backs."

"If I had that kind of spare cash, I'd do it," I tell her. Setting my glass down, I stand up and make my way to the fireplace. I put on a couple of fresh logs and kindling before using the lighter on the mantle to get it going.

Once the flame catches, I go back to the couch and tell Ashlyn, "I had a visitor today."

"Let me guess, seventy bears showed up because they heard you were giving away granola."

"Uh, no." *Thank goodness.* "Allegra was here."

"In Maple Falls?" Ashlyn sounds as surprised by her audacity as I was.

"Yup. She was outside of Shirley May's when I came out."

"What did she want?" Ashlyn looks displeased, and I can't help but hope she's also the tiniest bit jealous.

"She asked me to go back to New York with her and give her another chance."

The muscles in Ashlyn's face appear to sag in unison. "Oh."

"I told her that I lived in Maple Falls now and I wasn't going back to New York."

She raises her chin just enough that our eyes connect. "Does that mean she's moving here?"

"What? No! I'm not getting back together with her. I told her we were through."

Ashlyn looks relieved. "How did she take that?"

"It obviously wasn't what she wanted to hear, but she seemed to accept it. I expect she went right to the airport and got on the first plane out of here."

"Wow. Okay. I mean, I guess I'm glad for you that you got closure."

"I didn't need closure," I remind her.

"Maybe so, but I think it was good for you to see Allegra again. Just so you know for sure."

"I knew for sure when she called me from Martinique and told me she wasn't coming home. I didn't need to see her to know there was no coming back from that."

Ashlyn kicks off her shoes before putting her feet up on the coffee table. "Did you feel anything when you saw her?"

"I guess I felt a little bit sorry for her," I say. "But I mainly felt like I didn't know her anymore. Does that make sense?"

Ashlyn's head bobs up and down. "I dated a guy for five months once. One night, when we weren't getting together, I went to a Dodgers game with some girlfriends. Turns out, he was there with two other guys and three women. It looked like they were on a group date."

"Creep," I say for lack of anything else coming to mind.

"Yeah, but the thing was, that even though I knew it was

him, he didn't seem like the man I knew. It was like I was watching a total stranger."

"How so?" I ask, intrigued to hear her answer.

Shrugging, she itemizes, "He laughed differently. He held his head differently. He even parted his hair on the other side."

"Maybe the guy you were dating had a twin," I suggest.

She snorts. "I thought the same thing! But I took out my phone and texted him to see what he'd do."

Taking off my own shoes, I follow her lead and put my feet up. "What happened?"

"As soon as I sent my text, he pulled his phone out of his pocket and read it. Then he ignored it and went back to his date."

"Ouch."

"You'd think I would have wanted to go up to him and call him out, but I didn't. I had this overwhelming sensation that I was receiving a warning, and I should take it to heart. This guy wasn't the one for me."

There are so many people who aren't on the up and up, it makes me sick. Trying to make light of a tough situation, I say, "I bet he wasn't from Utah."

Ashlyn's laugh comes out like a bark. "You got that right." Then she teases me right back. "He was probably from New York City."

"He was probably from LA."

"Maybe so," she says. "So, anyway, no more Allegra, huh?"

I shake my head. "I've been telling you that all along. You just didn't believe me."

Ashlyn finishes her glass of champagne in one gulp like she's trying to gather her courage. "I know what Allegra Johansen looks like, Jamie. She's the most gorgeous woman I've ever seen."

"What does that have to do with anything?"

"I just think it would be hard to let a woman like that go."

"Who's the most handsome male movie star you can think of?" I ask her.

"Henry Cavill." She doesn't even pause before answering.

"Say you and Henry dated for three years …"

She doesn't let me finish before interrupting. "Impossible."

"Why?"

"Because I would never date a guy like that for so long before proposing to him."

Her candor makes me smile. "You'd propose to him?"

"It's Henry Cavill, Jamie. Of course I'd propose to him."

I bet she would, too. "Fine. Say you and Henry had been dating for a year when he went away to make a movie."

She shakes her head again.

"What now?" I ask.

"I wouldn't let him go away without me. I'd want to protect my interests."

"Let me try this again. You and Henry are away on vacation, and you catch him flirting with a waitress. What do you do?"

"I tell him to stop it," she says.

"And what if he tells you he's been secretly seeing her and that he won't stop?"

The outrage on her face is clear. "I'd tell him to take a hike!"

"Even though he's the most gorgeous man you've ever met?" Feeling the need to tease her, I add, "Present company excluded, of course."

The nodding of her head picks up speed. "Fine, I get it. Looks have nothing to do with the quality of person. But even so, Allegra is a knockout."

"A knockout who treated me like dirt," I remind her.

Ashlyn takes a big breath before saying, "I'm glad you're not going to get back together with her."

"Really? Because it started to feel like you were trying to talk me into it."

While staring at her lap, she tells me, "You're too good for her. You deserve to find a woman who knows what a catch you are."

"Do you think that woman might be here in Maple Falls?" I'm hoping she'll say yes.

But instead of giving me the answer I want, she utters, "I suppose it's possible." And while that isn't the definitive response I was looking for, it's not a no.

Now that we know Ashlyn's parents are safe, I say a silent prayer they don't return home before I can win their daughter over.

CHAPTER 29
ASHLYN

JAMIE HAYES SHOULD COME with a warning. Something along the lines of, *This man may cause your knees to buckle, your heart to beat in overdrive, and your imagination to take wild flights of fancy.*

Sitting on his sofa drinking champagne with him last night made me feel secure and reckless at the same time. But mostly reckless. So much so that I made a lame excuse to leave after only one glass. Had I stayed any longer, I might have thrown myself at him and begged him to love me.

I'm proud I didn't do that. At thirty-two years of age, I've learned not to take stupid risks regarding members of the opposite sex. Those risks include getting involved with men who've had a sketchy work history—I'm no one's sugar mama; falling for a guy who's recently broken up with a long-term girlfriend— I've been the rebound girl and will not do it again; and finally, I will not date geographically undesirables. The longest distance relationship I ever tried was with a guy who lived in San Diego and believe me when I tell you, there's nothing romantic about sitting in traffic hoping to get to your destination before midnight.

So far, Jamie is two out of three on my "Don't" list. He might say he's over Allegra, but the woman came to Maple Falls on a quest to win him back. That says how determined she is, and quite frankly, I don't know him well enough to go to war for him. Which brings me to the fact that he lives in Washington, which is like ten times farther away than San Diego.

I know I said I'd go to the Ice Breakers inaugural bash with Jamie tonight, but I'm currently trying to devise a believable enough excuse to get out of it.

Trying to take my mind off my worries, I scroll through my dad's messages and return as many of them as I have the answers for. I don't respond to the twelve from Phillip. I've tried everything, including a fake snake infestation, to get that guy off my back, but he's apparently the most determined mayoral assistant on the planet. He's like the superhero of nerds with no risk of Marvel ever reenacting his life on film because his only power is that he's massively annoying.

Next, I check my texts. The first one is from my landlord, and it sends shivers of dread up my spine.

> HABIB BROCK
>
> Hey Ashlyn, I'm not sure if you've been watching the news but the Hollyway fire is heading in your direction. There's no threat of evacuation yet, but you might want to pack a bag just in case.

The Hollyway fire? What in the world? After a quick Google search, I discover while I've been trying to save Maple Falls, three different fires have started in Los Angeles. That may sound like a lot, but October is fire season in LA. As such, it's likely that a dozen fires will start and most will be put out before becoming a danger to anyone.

I've personally been evacuated from two different rentals in the last ten years, and my possessions have remained untouched by disaster. Even so, I figure, I'd better talk to someone on the ground and see how things are going.

I hit the button with my friend Amber's face on it and wait for her to answer. She doesn't, so I try my friend Callie.

Callie picks up after one ring. "I've been thinking about you since I got up, but we just got the word that we're the next block to be evacuated." Callie only lives two miles from me.

"Cal, I'm in Washington. I'm not even home." I'm starting to sense that my life is turning into Dante's third ring of hell. First with the Maple Falls disaster—which is how I view Alexander MacDonald—then my parents getting hit with a hurricane, and now my house is in a potential fire path. I must have been an evil dictator in a past life.

"Dillion, get the cat in the crate!" Callie shouts. "I've got his food packed, but you need to get him before he crawls under the bed, and we can't get him out." Then she tells me, "I need to go. There are a million things to do, and I don't want to leave behind anything important."

"Is it that bad?" Angelinos are notoriously unruffled in the face of disaster. We handle earthquakes like they're a fun ride, fires like a BBQ opportunity, and riots like another Friday night. As such, her obvious anxiety has me on edge.

"Honey," Callie says, "it's not good."

"Should I come home?"

"If the Santa Anas shift in your direction, you'll never make it in time. If they don't, you'll be fine."

"Do you want to go to my house?" I ask her. "My landlord says there's no word of evacuation yet."

Callie is quiet for a minute before she says, "You know what? Yes. We were going to go to Dillion's parents' in Pasadena, but Sammy hates their dog. Is your key still under the planter?"

"Yup," I tell her. Not only am I happy to help a friend, but I'm relieved to know someone will be watching out for my stuff. "Keep me posted on any new developments," I tell her.

"Will do. Gotta go." She hangs up abruptly.

All thoughts of trying to get out of going to the ball tonight leave my head. Jamie is comforting in a crisis and right now I could use some of that.

Getting into the shower, I give myself permission to have a wonderful time tonight without caring that Jamie can never be the one for me. Heck, I'll be too busy worrying about the fires in LA to add him to the list.

After standing under the rain dial for long minutes, I dry off and do my hair before putting on my makeup. I was only planning to be here for a week, so I didn't bring any nice dresses. Checking out my mom's closet, I find two possibilities. A silky red number with a plunging neckline and a high slit, and a black cocktail dress with a scooped back. I'm in awe my mom has kept her figure in such good shape and can only hope that I'm still wearing dresses like this when I'm her age.

I decide to go with the red dress because it's more of a standout, and even though Jamie and I aren't dating for real, I want to make him proud. After finding a matching pair of shoes, I dig through my mom's jewelry box and accessorize with her gold and ruby earrings. My life in LA is way more casual than this so I feel like I'm playing dress-up like I did when I was a kid.

Looking at the clock, I realize I have a half-hour before Jamie picks me up. I consider popping over to see Clara, but thirty minutes is no time to catch up with an old friend. Also, I might see her at the event tonight.

I'm about to sit out front on the porch swing to wait when my phone rings. "Hello?"

"Ashlyn, it's me," Jamie says.

"Hey. Are you almost here?" I wonder why he's calling right before picking me up.

"About that … No, I'm still home."

"Well, get moving, buddy. I'm all dressed up with no place to go."

"Would you mind going to the store?" he asks, sounding nervous.

"Jamie, what's going on?" Whatever he needs, he can surely get it on his way to pick me up.

"I need about twenty boxes of granola," he announces.

"Why?" Even as I ask I start to have a vague suspicion.

"Remember how you told me not to feed the bears because they would bring their friends?"

"Oh, no!" I can't help it, I start laughing. "How many are there?"

"Ten? Twenty? It's hard to say. There could be a hundred for all I know."

"And you want me to come over and feed them?"

He pauses for a beat. "That probably wouldn't be safe, huh?"

"I'm not worried about my safety," I tell him. "I'll be in a car. If it feels dangerous, I'll just leave."

"Then you'll come?" He sounds so relieved, I can't help the smile that comes to my face.

"Of course I'll come. But the grocery store probably won't have that much granola. I'll have to improvise."

"I don't care what you bring. Just get as much granola as you can for the original three. The newbies don't have any expectations yet."

"Do you need anything for yourself?" I ask.

"How about a pizza?"

"I think they're going to feed us at the ball," I tell him. "Unless the pizza is just an appetizer."

"Ashlyn," Jamie says my name with the same tone he might use if he were about to confess to a crime. "I can't leave here."

"What do you mean you're not leaving? I thought we were going to the Ice Breakers inaugural ball?"

"I should go," he says. "But there's no way I can walk through all those bears. No way. I'm trying to be brave here, but I've got to tell you I'm terrified. I even considered calling the police, but I'm afraid this whole thing would get out and then in addition to being Allegra's jilted boyfriend, I'll be the man being held hostage by bears. I don't think I could handle the ridicule."

Jamie Hayes is simply adorable. I know he feels like a coward, but I don't know anyone who could easily walk through a bunch of bears. "Don't worry about tonight," I tell him. "Hibernation is coming any time now and you'll be left alone until the spring."

"I have to move out before they wake up," he says anxiously. "You don't think they'll try to break into my cabin, do you?"

"I think you should lock your windows and doors, just in case." Then I tell him, "Depending on how many there are, we may still have to call for reinforcements."

"I know. I just didn't want to come off as hysterical and I thought you might be a better judge of things. But only if you're okay with that."

"I'm good," I tell him while picking up my purse. "I'll bring supper and bear food. We can assess the situation once I get there."

"Ashlyn …" Jamie starts to speak but he doesn't finish his sentence.

"Yes?"

"Thank you. I feel like a real chicken and you're the only person I could think of that I wasn't embarrassed to call. The guys on the team would have a field day if they knew."

"I'm honored," I tell him sincerely. "And I won't tell a soul." I can't help myself from teasing him, "You know, unless we need to call in the National Guard or something."

"Ha, ha. Let's start with the cereal and go from there." He pauses a beat before adding, "Please hurry."

"On my way," I tell him.

I stop off in the pantry and grab a couple of cans of my dad's bear spray, even though I don't really think I'll need them. I'm pretty sure Jamie is overreacting, but it's better safe than sorry.

Grabbing my keys, I head out to my car. First stop, cereal. Second stop, grown man locked in his cabin quaking in fear because of all the new friends he's inadvertently made.

CHAPTER 30
JAMIE

I REALIZE I've hit a new low point in life as I hurry to the front door to make sure it's locked. Once that task is accomplished, I make my way around the cabin and check the latches on all the windows. I am literally surrounded by bears. Luckily, no one seems aggressive, but that doesn't mean the threat isn't there. All it will take is for one to attack to encourage them all.

My next course of action—if you can call it action being that I'm trapped indoors—is to pull all the food out of the kitchen cabinets. I'll have to do something to placate my visitors should it take Ashlyn awhile to get here. Unfortunately, all I have is a handful of energy bars, a sack of bagels, and a bag of chips. Beads of sweat pop up along my hairline as I imagine the headline that might run with this story. "Pro Hockey Player Killed for Cereal!" Or how about, "Hungry Bears Turn Rogue and Eat Captain of the Ice Breakers." *How is this my life?*

While I'd like nothing more than to crawl into bed and pull the covers over my head, I'm afraid if I don't keep a close eye on my visitors, they'll combine their efforts and break in. Which is why I keep walking from room to room assessing the situation. After twenty minutes, I realize they're slowly moving closer to the cabin.

Ashlyn arrives with a toot of her horn which causes the bears to turn around and look her way. Nobody runs, so I figure the whole loud noise thing isn't going to work on them anymore. Looks like all the screaming I'll be doing will be for naught. But don't get me wrong, I'll still be doing it.

I watch Ashlyn open her car door and get out. I want to call to her and tell her it's not worth the risk, and that she should run, but at the same time, I'm totally mesmerized by the sight of her. She's wearing the most amazingly sexy dress I have ever seen. It's almost enough to get me to run out of this house and go to the ball with her. I would surely be the envy of all to have her on my arm.

Opening the door a crack, I hear Ashlyn tell the local bear community, "So you decided to have a party and not invite me, huh?" Her accompanying giggle sounds like wind chimes tinkling in the distance.

Obviously, the bears don't answer her, but they all appear to be as captivated by her presence as I am.

Ashlyn goes around her car and opens the back door. She removes several grocery bags which she drapes over her arms. Then she walks away from the house toward the woods. *What is she doing?*

I'm about to ask her when she stops and empties one of the bags on the ground. Three cereal boxes hit the dirt. Ashlyn puts her other bags down before opening the three and meticulously scatters them around. Several bears start to make their way in her direction. Picking up the rest of the groceries, she walks to the other side of the woods where she repeats the process. She zigzags three more times, all the while gently talking to the curious onlookers. Then she heads toward the porch. On her way, she runs into my biggest op. The OG papa bear.

Old papa stands on his hind legs and roars so loud I'm about to run out and sacrifice myself for Ashlyn's safety. She must sense this because she looks up at me and says, "Slow your roll, Jamie. I've got this."

She dumps her last bag of cereal boxes out before picking them up and chucking the whole lot of them into the woods. My nemesis immediately turns and follows the trajectory of his supper.

Once the path is clear, Ashlyn hurries to the door, pushing me aside to gain entrance. "You weren't kidding when you said you'd been invaded! I counted sixteen."

"You were amazing," I tell her. "You didn't seem afraid at all."

She looks up at me with a spooked expression. "I was terrified."

"You didn't look it."

"I made a huge mistake," she says while pushing past me and flopping onto the couch. She creates enough wind that the slit in her skirt blows open and gives me an unhindered view of her toned legs. *Wow!*

"What mistake?" I ask. "Because from where I was standing, it looked like you totally had the situation under control."

Her head shakes slowly from side to side, causing her hair to move like a silk curtain dancing in the breeze. "I gave them *all* the food. I was planning to hold some back for when we left but I panicked and gave them everything."

"Even our supper?" As she came in empty-handed, I'm guessing that's the case.

"Yup. You got anything left in here?"

"A couple protein bars, some bagels, and a bag of chips."

She throws her head back against the pillows. "This is why you don't feed bears, Jamie."

"I see that now," I tell her humbly. "We should probably call the cops, huh? Or animal control? Maybe the Navy?"

She releases an exasperated groan. Let's give them time to fill their bellies. They'll have to go to sleep at some point and that will be our best opportunity to escape."

"When do they usually sleep?" I ask.

She picks up her phone to look up the answer to my question. "Looks like they knock off an hour or two after sunset. But hopefully, they'll be so stuffed they'll get drowsy sooner."

Walking into the kitchen, I grab two energy bars before joining her in the living room. I hand her one and say, "I don't know about you, but even if we get out of here in decent time, I don't think I'm up to making an appearance at the ball."

"Fine by me," she replies with relief in her voice. "I probably sweated right through my dress anyway."

Sitting down next to her, I tell her, "You look beautiful."

A soft smile forms on her mouth. "Thank you. You look pretty nice yourself." She adds, "I'm surprised you have a tux."

Instead of playing it off like I'm as cool as 007, I confess, "It's a rental."

"A very nice one."

Neither one of us speaks for several moments and the silence becomes thick. "Thank you again for saving me," I finally say.

Her head bobs briefly in recognition of my compliment. Then she announces, "My house in LA might be about to burn down."

"Excuse me?"

She takes a small bite of her energy bar and chews it thoughtfully before answering. "My landlord texted me. I didn't even know my area was in danger."

"Southern California is as close to the Book of Revelations as anywhere on the planet. I mean earthquakes, fires, floods … it's a lot."

"It's so beautiful though," she says. "It rarely gets below fifty degrees and the sun shines ninety percent of the time …"

"Which is why you're in a drought," I interrupt.

"Yeah. But after growing up in Washington, I've found that I really love the sun."

"You don't have much humidity in LA, either." It sounds like I'm changing camps.

"And the food is out of this world," she adds.

"You've got great beaches."

"Lots of good hiking."

"You don't ever think you'll leave, huh?" In the back of my mind, I suppose I was hoping that Ashlyn would move back to Maple Falls, and we could give our budding interest in each other a chance to grow. It looks like I'll have to accept that isn't going to happen.

"I've made a nice life for myself," she says. "I have a great business, and a stellar reputation. Which of course keeps my business growing."

"But the dating is abysmal," I remind her.

"True. But there's always Utah," she jokes. "And there are no bears in my neighborhood. Coyotes are my biggest wildlife concern."

"Are they dangerous?" I want to know.

"Not unless you're a small child or dog," she says. My eyes must bug out because she assures me, "People there know not to leave either unattended."

I love how comfortably Ashlyn and I banter back and forth. There's an ease with her that I've only felt with my really good friends. I guess that's exactly what we're becoming to one another—good friends.

"We have rats the size of house cats in New York City," I tell her. "And roaches the size of rats."

Her face contorts in horror. "I would drop dead on the spot if I saw either."

"I guess it's a matter of the devil you know," I tell her. Standing up, I ask, "Want a fire?"

"That would be nice." She lowers her eyes as though she's having thoughts she doesn't want me to see.

Walking over to the fireplace, I lay down new logs and kindling. Then I crumple up a newspaper and add it to the pile. After igniting the flame, I stand back and watch as it crackles to life. "How do you feel about dancing?" I ask her.

"What kind?" she wants to know. "Ballet? Hip Hop? Hula?"

I turn toward her while taking my phone out of my pocket. Then I connect to Spotify and start my Frank Sinatra playlist before answering, "I suppose you could hula, but I was hoping you might like to dance with me." I reach a hand toward her hopefully.

A million thoughts seem to flash across Ashlyn's face before she tentatively reaches out and takes my hand. "I do like to dance."

After helping her up, I gently pull her toward me. Once she's in my arms, I tell her, "We haven't known each other for a long time, but we sure have been through a lot together."

Snorting softly, she itemizes, "The potential downfall of Maple Falls, my parents getting caught in a hurricane, my house being in the line of fire …"

I add my own drama to the list. "The return of my ex and averting a bear attack. At least for now ..."

While Frank's dulcet tones fill the air around us, Ashlyn gently lays her head on my shoulder. I can't help myself; I lean down and inhale the fragrance emanating from her hair. The light floral scent is intoxicating. "What do you say we forget about everything for now and try to enjoy ourselves?"

She releases a low groan of contentment. "That sounds nice."

I know I signed a contract with the Ice Breakers, and I'm legally bound to play with them, but I can't help but wonder if they might trade me to Los Angeles. I have a sneaking feeling my future happiness might all be resting on the shoulders of the woman I'm dancing with.

CHAPTER 31
ASHLYN

AS LUCK WOULD HAVE IT, Jamie and I didn't have to run for our lives when we left his cabin last night. We fed his neighbors to the point they happily left to find their beds a short time after eating. Once that happened, Jamie packed a suitcase, and we headed to our cars.

Jamie was going to check into the lodge, but I suggested he stay at my parents' house with me. I'm currently lying in bed wondering why I did that. I have a hard enough time being around the man without adding obstacles like sleeping in the room right next door to his.

Grabbing my phone, I check my messages to see if there's any news from LA. The only text is from Callie.

CALLIE

> Hey, girl. We're at your house but I'm not sure how much longer we can stay here. The fire has moved and is only a mile away, but at least the wind changed direction. If I were you, I'd grab the first flight out. You might have time to pack up some stuff in case the worst happens.

I call my friend immediately. "This is actually terrifying," I tell her as soon as she answers the phone.

"It's bad," she agrees. "I mean, we both know people who have lost everything, but it's a different animal when it's happening to you."

"What do you think the odds are that my house will make it?" I ask her.

Callie blows out her breath loudly into the phone. "Ash, my house burned down last night."

"No! Oh, Cal, I'm so sorry!"

"Me, too." The quiver in her voice causes the short hairs on my arms to stand at attention. "So, to answer your question, I don't think the odds are in your favor. Come home."

I throw the covers off and jump out of bed. "I'm on my way," I tell her. "I'll keep you posted on when I'll arrive."

"Be safe," she says before hanging up.

I yank my nightgown off before putting on a pair of jeans and a sweater. Then instead of brushing my hair, I simply pull it back into a ponytail.

Grabbing my purse, I walk out of my room. I pass the guest room where Jamie's sleeping and give the open door a brief knock to get his attention.

He rolls over in bed before sitting up. *Great, he's not wearing a shirt.* My Pavlovian response is to start salivating. "Good morning," he says in a gravelly and very sexy morning voice.

"I'm heading back to LA," I tell him. "I'm going to try to save some of my stuff."

Throwing his legs over the side of the bed, he says, "I'll go with you."

"You can't," I remind him. "Your first game is coming up in a couple of days."

He runs his hands through his hair which causes it to stand on end in a comical way. "Shoot. I don't think you should go alone."

"I'll be fine," I tell him. "I've lived there for over a decade. I know how to navigate the dangers."

He grabs a t-shirt off the nightstand and puts it on. "At least let me drive you to the airport. When does your flight leave?"

"I don't have one yet," I tell him. "I was just going to get there and find one."

"Go make some coffee. I'll be right down. You can book the flight while I drive."

"Jamie." I start to tell him that he doesn't have to take me, but I stop myself because I really want him to. "Thank you. It seems we're always coming to each other's aid, huh?"

"That's what good friends, do," he says. His voice is tinged with something that, if I didn't know better, I might call longing.

With a small smile, I turn and leave his room. Once I'm in the kitchen, I start a pot of coffee brewing before putting a couple of bagels into the toaster. After they pop up, I smear them with cream cheese and wrap them in paper towels to take with us. Then I fill two thermoses with coffee. To mine, I add my favorite hazelnut creamer and a stevia packet.

Jamie walks into the room moments later looking like he's just stepped off the cover of *GQ* magazine. Seriously, he looks effortlessly gorgeous. I point to his thermos. "It's just coffee, but you can add whatever you want to it."

Screwing the lid on, he tells me, "I like it black."

I hand him his bagel and lead the way out of the house. "You want to take my car or yours?"

"Let's take mine," he says.

Once we're situated inside, he pulls out of the driveway and heads toward the outskirts of town. I open up my phone and start looking for a flight. "There's one that leaves in an hour and a half," I tell him after a short search. "That ought to be enough time."

"It's a good thing you don't have to check any luggage."

"Yeah." It's not that I don't love talking to Jamie, but right now, my head is so full of fear, I don't have much to say. He seems to sense this because he stays quiet, as well.

An hour later, he turns onto the airport road. "I wish I could go in with you, but as it is, you'll have to run if you're gonna make your flight." He pulls up to the curb and puts the car into park. Then he turns to me and says, "Be careful."

Faking bravado I don't feel, I tell him, "I will. Fate didn't let us become friends only for me to burn up in a fire." The look of horror on his face is immediate. So, I assure him, "They won't even let me near my house if there's a threat."

That information seems to calm him. Opening his door, he gets out and runs around the SUV to open mine. I take his offered hand and let him help me down the high step to the ground. He doesn't let my hand go once I'm standing in front of him. Instead, he takes my other hand and pulls me toward him. "Call me as soon as you can."

I don't dare look up into his eyes or I'll probably never be able to leave. "I better go," I tell him, staring up at his hairline.

He still doesn't release my hands. Instead, he leans his face down toward mine and very gently kisses me. On the mouth. It's only a peck but molten heat starts to make its way through my nervous system. I'm pretty sure I'm about to spontaneously combust.

I force myself to give his hands a quick squeeze before releasing my grip. "I'll be fine," I assure him again. Then I turn around and make a run for it.

The line at security is longer than I was expecting, so I do the thing that I hate. I ask people if I can butt in front of them. Most are lovely and I wind up getting to my gate just as they're about to close the doors.

Handing my ticket to the agent, I tell him, "Sorry for being late."

He rolls his eyes. "Lady, no one wants to go to LA right now. I'm surprised you're even here."

After finding my seat, I look around the plane at all the faces. I wonder how many of them are hurrying home to do the same thing I am. Oddly, most people appear impassive. I usually admire that in my fellow Angelinos—you know, the ability to overcome any adversity without showing fear. We're a people known for meeting any challenge with a stoicism others might find shocking.

Having said that, I don't currently find my fellow travelers' inexpressiveness particularly appealing. Instead, I view it as almost robotic, as though emotion is something they're not capable of. I spend the entire flight wondering at this change in my perception. Maybe it's because I'm in a fight-or-flight frame of mind. But then again it might be that I just don't relate to them anymore. I shelve that thought for later evaluation.

As soon as the plane lands, I text Callie.

ME

You still at my house?

CALLIE

Still here. The fires are holding their distance.

ME

I just landed. I'll hop in an Uber and with any luck I'll be there in an hour.

CALLIE

See you then.

I run through LAX like I'm in hot pursuit of my favorite french fries. When I get outside, I discover the Uber line is long. Panicked, I shout, "I need to get to my house before it's evacuated. Can I please cut in line?"

I'm met with a wide variety of nos. One woman glares at me and says, "I have an audition. I can't be late for that." The man in front of her adds, "We all have problems, honey. You're going to have to wait your turn."

I look around, wildly wondering if I should try to rent a car, but there's no telling how long that could take. That's when I notice the back window of a nearby limo rolling down. A stunningly good-looking man pops his head out. "Where are you headed?"

I'm not one to take a ride from a stranger, but there's something about this guy that seems familiar. I give him the address, and he says, "I can drop you. I'm on the way to the hospital. My wife is in labor."

I don't want to keep him from his wife, but I'm also not one to look a gift horse in the mouth. The door opens so I hop in next to him. "Thank you so much," I say. "I didn't even know the fires were so bad." Then I ramble like a total idiot. "I was in Washington and was preoccupied with all the troubles in Maple Falls, and I just …"

"Maple Falls?" he asks. "Why were you in Maple Falls?"

"I'm from there," I tell him. "Do you know it?"

He looks shocked. "I met my wife there. My brother lives there."

Talk about a small world. "Who's your brother?"

"Troy Hart," he says. "He owns the …"

"Ice Breakers!" I say excitedly. No wonder he looked familiar. "Troy's been very helpful helping us raise money."

He sticks his hand out to shake mine. "Zach Hart," he says. "I've heard about your troubles."

Zach Hart? This guy is a billionaire! Before I can beg him to help us—especially as his wife is from Maple Falls— he offers, "I'd be happy to contribute to the cause if you can't make your number." Then he pulls out a business card and hands it to me.

I'm not sure if Zach is good for it or not, but what are the chances *he* would offer *me* a ride. I'm starting to think Jamie might be onto something with his beliefs about fate. I mean, there's no way any of this is happening by chance.

CHAPTER 32
JAMIE

I HATE that Ashlyn is in LA and I'm in Maple Falls. She's been great about calling and texting updates, but even so, the size of the fire has grown significantly in the last few days. The last time I talked to her was this morning when she told me the winds had shifted again. She's been alerted evacuation is imminent. If the Ice Breakers didn't have their first game tonight, I would be by her side instead of on my way to the arena.

Driving up to the stadium, I have to temporarily put my worry for Ashlyn on the back burner. I slowly allow the thrill of game day to build inside of me, and before long I feel like I'm a kid about to take the ice for the first time. I hurriedly park and walk through the locker room entrance.

My old teammate Cade Lenox is the first person I run into. As a new team, we truly lucked out getting a star winger like him. "Hey, man," I say. "You ready to rock this thing?"

He looks up from his task of putting on his pads. "I'm in the mood to smack some pucks."

"And any fool stupid enough to get in your way?" This was something we used to always say when we played for New York.

"You know it," he says with a determined grin.

Asher Tremblay joins us. As far as defensemen go, he's one of the top dogs in the league. "Is it strange that I'm a little nervous?" he wants to know.

Shaking my head, I tell him, "Nerves show you still care."

His nostrils flare as he says, "This is why you're the captain. You're like our very own cheerleader."

I'm glad he sees it that way, because right now, I'm still torn between staying here and flying off to LA to offer Ashlyn my support.

Once we're all geared up, I lead the team out onto the boards. Dale is waiting for us, and "Ice, Ice, Baby" is booming through the loudspeakers, doing its job to ramp up the already electrified atmosphere.

"You guys ready to let the world know who the Ice Breakers are?" our coach asks. He smiles with borderline glee. Dale is not known to show great emotion during a game, so it's clear how excited he is.

Looking at me, he passes the metaphorical baton. "You have anything you want to say to the team, Jamie?"

"Yeah, I have something to say." I take a beat to catch everyone's eye. "Most of us don't know each other very well yet, but our shared love of this game has made it clear we're a force to be reckoned with. Let's get out there and show the doubters we're on a mission to take the cup." Putting my hand into the center of the group, I wait for the others to follow suit. "Ice Breakers on three," I tell them before counting down.

Once we've declared our battle cry, the starting lineup hits the ice. As I glide to the center for the puck drop, I feel the anticipation building in the stands like I'm the one singing the National Anthem at the Super Bowl.

When the puck falls, I feint back like I'm going to let the other team get it, but then at the last second I shoot my stick out and grab it. I immediately turn and send it flying down the ice to Asher Tremblay, or Mr. Sunshine as I teasingly call him. Seriously, the guy always has a smile on his face.

Asher takes possession with the ease of someone born with a hockey stick in his hands. He moves effortlessly, the puck dancing on the blade of his stick like it's magnetized. The crowd roars with every stride he takes toward the opposing team's goal.

True to their reputation, the Great Lake Vikings aren't making it easy on him. Two defensemen surge toward him, their sticks slashing at the ice as they close in. Yet, Asher doesn't panic. He rapidly changes course, pulling the puck with him. The defensemen lunge to block his path, but he cuts sharply to the right and leaves them in his dust.

Meanwhile, the goalie is waiting and watching, crouched low and ready to pounce. Asher keeps his gaze steady, and his focus unyielding, as he nears the net. A player from the opposing team barrels toward him from the side, intent on bodychecking him into the next county, but Asher anticipates the move. He spins out of reach, as fast as a ninja dropping from the sky.

Miraculously, he keeps the puck secure the entire time. The noise from the stands is deafening and seemingly shakes the very ice beneath our skates. Asher slows just enough to draw the goalie away from his post. Then, in one smooth motion, he slaps the puck with a sharp, calculated arc. It rockets past the goalie's outstretched glove and slams into the back of the net with a resounding clang. The arena explodes with excitement as the bench erupts into our new war cry. "Ice Breakers! Ice Breakers! Ice Breakers!"

Asher pumps his fist into the air as he glides back toward the team. "That's how we do it people!" he shouts, his voice barely audible over the pandemonium. The rest of the first period is just as thrilling, and the Ice Breakers prove they are a new power-house in the NHL.

I rotate out in the middle of the second period to let another player come in. In my early years, I resented any time I wasn't in the fray, but now that I'm in my mid-thirties, I've earned the right to an occasional break.

As soon as my butt hits the wood, I look up at the Jumbotron and my jaw nearly hits the floor. The camera is focused right on Allegra's face. *What is she doing here?*

I look over at Harry, whose eyes are also trained on the screen. He glances my way and asks, "You two back together?"

"We are not," I tell him sternly.

"Why's she here, then?"

A slow heat starts to flow through me as my heartbeat picks up speed. "I have no idea."

"She must be here for you," he says. "And no hate, but you'd be an idiot not to get back with her."

I stare at Harry for a long moment, trying to assess his intent. Is he trying to get me to go back to her so I'll look like an idiot in front of the whole world? I can't tell. So I say, "Allegra and I are through. She made her feelings clear, and I'm not going back for another round of 'make Jamie look like a fool.'"

Harry nods his head slowly. "I get it, man. I really do." That's when I realize he doesn't appear to have a hidden agenda. He's on the up and up. But then he adds, "If you're not interested, do you mind if I throw my hat in the ring?" I can't help but wonder if he thinks by dating Allegra he'll somehow even the score between us. But either way, it's no skin off my nose.

"Do what you want," I tell him. "Just remember Allegra can be dangerous when she has possession of your heart."

"Warning heard loud and clear," Harry says. Changing the subject, he adds, "We're killing it out there, Hayes."

A slow smile forms as I concur. "We sure are, Franks. We sure are."

The rest of the game whizzes by like time has no meaning, and we take it 3-0. Once we return to the locker room, bottles of champagne get shaken and popped as we all dance around celebrating our first win as a team.

As much as I want to party with the guys, there's one person's voice I can't wait another minute to hear. Grabbing my phone out of my locker, I make my way to Dale's abandoned office. Then I sit down and call Ashlyn.

"Hey," I say as soon as she answers.

"Hey, yourself. How was the game?"

"You didn't watch, huh?" I tease. I know there's nothing but fire on her mind.

"We just evacuated," she says. "I'm heading to Pasadena to Callie's husband's parents' house."

"Oh, Ashlyn, I'm so sorry. Is there anything I can do?" I ask, even though I know there isn't.

"You could have a chat with fate if you want and put in a good word for me."

"I hate to say this, but what if it's fate for your house to burn down?"

Her gasp makes me sorry I asked. "To what end?"

"I don't know," I tell her. "But it happens to a lot of people where you live, and I'm pretty sure it leads them to a new phase in life."

"An eviction notice would be easier," she says, sounding defeated.

"I wish I could be there with you. I know it wouldn't change the course of the fire, but it sure would make me feel better."

"You've got another game tomorrow," she says. "You need to stay put. By the way, you never told me if you won tonight."

"Oh, we won. It was a shutout, too." I kick my feet up onto Dale's desk and lean back in his chair.

"I don't know what that means."

"It means the other team didn't even score. I'm going to have to teach you about hockey when you get back," I tell her.

"About that …"

A wave of apprehension hits me. "What about that?"

"I talked to my parents and they're coming home tomorrow."

I know I should be happy her folks are able to get out of Barbados, but I'm not. "What does that mean for you?" I want to know.

"It means I don't need to be in Maple Falls anymore." Before I can protest, she says, "I'm a week late starting a new job as it is, but I talked to my client today and she's going to let me start tomorrow."

"Tomorrow? She should let you wait until you know your house is safe. Plus, don't you need to come back and fill your dad in on what's going on with the town?"

"I'm sure Phillip will do that, but I've also asked Marcy to be on hand, so my dad gets the facts straight. Phillip will probably make it sound like it's all my fault."

I'm having difficulty accepting the news that Ashlyn isn't coming back. "Are you saying when we said goodbye at the airport, that was it? I won't see you again?" I sound like a hurt puppy, but darn it, that's exactly how I feel.

"I'll visit my parents at some point. And maybe if you come to town for a game, we could grab dinner or something." She doesn't sound nearly as upset by our separation as I am.

"What about Maple Fest? It starts the day after tomorrow. You promised to show me around and tell me all the best stuff to eat."

"All the food is good, Jamie. Trust me, you can't go wrong with anything."

I feel like I've been jilted all over again, which is ridiculous because Ashlyn and I were never dating. "I'll miss you," I finally tell her. "You're my best friend in Maple Falls."

"I'll miss you, too," she says quietly. "But I'd better get going. I want to check for updates on the fire."

And just like that, my dream of convincing Ashlyn to stay in Maple Falls dies. She's made it clear that LA is her home, and I'm nothing more than a "buddy" to catch supper with if I show up in her domain.

How depressing.

CHAPTER 33
ASHLYN

I FEEL horrible about lying to Jamie about the reason I'm not coming back to Maple Falls. The truth is, my job doesn't start for two more weeks. But I knew if I went back to Washington I might never be able to leave. Also, I need to figure out where I'm going to live if the fire takes my current rental.

I slow my car down at the end of my road, and a fireman posted there motions for me to roll down my window. When I do, he tells me, "Once you leave, you won't be allowed back in until the threat passes."

"I know," I tell him.

"Are you sure you have everything?" He's making it clear he doesn't think there will be anything to come back to.

"I have as much as I could fit in my car," I tell him.

"Animals are all secure?"

"No animals."

He steps aside, "Okay, then. Good luck," he says as he waves me on.

Good luck, indeed. I'm going to need more than luck. I could use a miracle right now.

I drive slowly as I take the twists and turns that lead me out of my neighborhood toward the freeway. The hillsides are burning around me, and the feeling is surreal. It's not like I haven't seen similar destruction in the last decade, but this is the first time it's affecting me so seriously.

Once I get onto the freeway, I merge onto the 134 toward Pasadena. I've always liked Pasadena and wonder if I might relocate there if necessary. But as most of my jobs are on the Westside I realize I'd probably be tripling my commute to work. Nothing about that sounds appealing.

As I drive through Glendale, my phone rings. I hit the button to answer it on Bluetooth.

"Hey." It's Jamie.

My throat tightens with emotion at the thought of not knowing when I'll see him again. "What's up?"

"I just wanted to let you know that I'll move out of your parents' tomorrow and into the lodge. I don't want to scare them by being here when they get home."

I totally forgot about him staying at my parents' house. How's that for distracted? "That's probably a good idea," I tell him. "I mean, I don't think they'd mind, but if they knew you were there, they might assume something had been going on between us."

"And then they'd demand you move home so I can make an honest woman out of you?" *Is it me or does he sound like he likes that idea?*

"My concern is more for you," I tell him. "My dad might throw punches first and ask questions later."

He teasingly asks, "What about your mom?"

"She would probably congratulate me on making such a catch."

"You think I'm a catch?" He sounds pleased at the thought.

Traffic slows, so I veer into a faster lane. "You know you're a catch," I tell him plainly. "Don't fish for a compliment."

"You're a catch too, Ashlyn." He sounds so sincere, bumps spring up on my arms.

"Thank you, that's nice of you to say."

"It's the truth."

"Well, then. We're both catches. If we're lucky we might both find a member of the opposite sex who appreciates us." A wave of pure jealously washes through me at the thought of the woman who's lucky enough to snag Jamie.

"Remember fate," he says cryptically.

"It's been on my mind quite a lot," I assure him.

"I mean, remember that things happen for a reason. Even if they don't make sense at the time."

"If you're talking about my house burning down, I do not accept that anything good can come from that."

"I'm talking about everything, Ashlyn. Everything that happens in our lives is a conductor for the next thing. That's all I'm saying."

"I'll keep that in mind." Getting off at the Colorado Street exit, I tell Jamie, "I need to go. I'll call you in a day or two, okay?"

"Call sooner if you need me," he says.

And with that, we hang up again. Talking to Jamie feels so normal and so right, I can't imagine not doing it multiple times a day for the rest of my life. But I also know that if I hear his voice that often, I'll only be bringing heartache on myself. And that's the last thing I need right now.

DILLION'S PARENTS are very welcoming and do their best to make me feel at home. The guest room they are letting me stay in is lovely, but even so, it's strange being so close to home without being home.

I have a hard time sleeping, but I finally conk out around three a.m. Which is why I'm still asleep at ten when my phone rings.

I groggily reach for it. "Hello?"

"Ashlyn!" It's my dad.

"Hey, Dad. Are you home?"

"We are. Just arrived an hour ago to the find the police at the door."

"Why were the police there?" *Seriously, what else could go wrong?*

"Phillip called them." He chuckles. "He started to worry that you were up to no good and he thought you might have done away with me and your mother."

That little poop. "Excuse me?"

"He says he's been texting me nonstop and when he didn't get a response after twenty-four hours, he figured something had happened to us."

"He didn't get a response because I was FedExing your phone back to you so it would be there when you got home."

"I figured it was something like that when I opened the envelope on the doorstep and found my phone."

"I don't know how you put up with that guy, Dad. He's a real piece of work." I grunt loudly before sitting up and fluffing the pillows behind me.

"He's probably going to be the next mayor of Maple Falls," he says.

"Do not underestimate the intelligence of my hometown," I retort. "What did you tell the police?"

"What do you think I told them? I told them we were just fine."

It occurs to me that he hasn't said anything about the whole Alexander MacDonald fiasco, so I ask, "Any chance you've been updated on what's been going on in town while you were away?"

My father laughs. *Laughs!* "Your mother caught me up to speed on the flight home."

"Are you furious with me?" I ask nervously.

"Why would I be upset with you? It sounds like you've done your best to put everything into motion to save Maple Falls. You've done a great job, honey."

"What if Alexander doesn't take the money?" I want to know.

"That would have nothing to do with you," he says. "If Mr. MacDonald doesn't take the money then we'll have to figure something else out. But just know I couldn't have done a better job than you did."

Tears unexpectedly fill my eyes. "Thanks, Dad. That's a really nice thing to say."

"It's the truth. I told you I thought you'd make an excellent mayor, and you've proven I was right."

"I'd be a much better mayor than Phillip," I feel the need to tell him.

"I agree," he says. "But being that Phillip actually wants the job and you don't, I'm guessing he's the one we'll be stuck with when my term ends."

"You have my sympathies," I say sourly. "Marcy is going to fill you in on the details of what we've put into place later today. Let me know if you have any questions."

"Will do. How are things there? Your house still standing?"

I pick up my phone and look for messages before answering, "I haven't heard anything yet. I'll keep you updated though." I hurry to ask, "How are things going with you and Mom? You guys back on track?"

"One hundred percent," he says. "I've been a pigheaded fool. Nothing and no one is as important to me as your mother, and I have you to thank for reminding me of that."

"I love you guys," I tell him. "I'd do anything for you."

"Well, you certainly have. You've saved our marriage and you've done your best to save Maple Falls. I owe you a lot."

"Thanks, Dad. I'm glad you guys are staying together."

"We're doing more than staying together," he says. "We're planning our next vacation. We're thinking three weeks in Italy over Christmas."

"Seriously?"

"You betcha! Your mom and I had so much fun in Barbados, we can't wait to go someplace else and make more memories."

I don't know who I'm talking to, but I suddenly suspect the man on the other end of the line isn't my father at all. "You were hit by a hurricane, Dad," I remind him.

"And it was invigorating! There's nothing like staring death in the face to remind you about what really matters in life. Like what you must be feeling now with your house in jeopardy."

As soon as I hear those words, I realize that I've been looking at this fire all wrong. I've been feeling sorry for myself, like I'm a victim of a horrible twist of fate. I should really be seeing this as an opportunity to make a change. I'm just not sure yet what kind of change that will be.

CHAPTER 34
JAMIE

SITTING out on the little patio off my room at the lodge, I try to assess how I currently feel about living in Maple Falls. I had my doubts about how I'd do during my first week here, but then Ashlyn took me under her wing and helped me start to feel a sense of community. The Ice Breakers' continued efforts to help raise money for the town are a big part of that, as well.

But now that Ashlyn is no longer here, I once again feel like a visitor on the moon. I remind myself that I still have the team, and the guys and I are getting closer every day. For instance, Carson and Asher have decided to share a rental house.

It helps that we won our second game, too. Being two for two is a nice way to start the season, and I have a strong feeling we'll just keep winning. And that's not just cockiness on my part, either. The Ice Breakers have a magical team chemistry the likes of which I've never seen before.

Today is the first day of Maple Fest and while I had planned to go, I was going to do that accompanied by Ashlyn. It's weird to think of being there without her. She hasn't called me back to tell me what's going on with her house, and while I don't want to be a bother, I really want her to keep me updated.

Pulling my phone out of my pocket, I call her.

"Hello?" Her voice is breathy like she just sprinted a mile.

"How's it going?" I ask.

"Jamie, hey. It's okay. Good, really."

When she doesn't elaborate beyond that, I ask, "How's your house?"

"Still here," she says. "They created a fire line a few blocks from me and managed to stop the spread. It's already at eighty percent contained, so it's only a matter of time before the whole thing is out."

I'm relieved for her but at the same time another, less altruistic, thought hits me. Had Ashlyn's house burned down, there was still a chance she might have come back to Maple Falls. Now there's not. "I'm happy for you," I tell her. And I am. I'm just not happy for me.

"Thank you. It's been a wild week for sure."

"Do fires usually last so long?" I ask.

"Not usually, but the Santa Ana winds have been stronger than normal, and the continued drought doesn't help." She adds, "There are also several other fires burning so resources are strained."

I honestly don't know why anyone lives there but I don't say that. Instead, I go with, "How's your new job?"

"My job? Oh, you know, it's fine."

Her answer makes me wonder if she really has a job. "I thought it started today."

"Uh, yeah. But I put it off until tomorrow. You know, just resettling back into my place."

Neither one of us says anything for a few beats and for the first time, I feel like I'm struggling to make small talk with Ashlyn. I finally tell her, "Maple Fest starts today."

"Yeah, I know. Have you gone yet?"

"No. The girl who was going to show me around had other plans." Even though I don't want to be petty, I'm still feeling a bit sorry for myself.

"What girl?" Is it me or is there a hint of jealousy in her tone?

Stretching my legs out in front of me, I take a sip of my coffee before telling her, "You."

"Oh. Yeah, well, I'm sorry about that."

"You could fly up today and still join me," I suggest. "I'm guessing your new client won't expect you in on the weekend."

"Jamie." She sighs my name like I'm an annoyance. "I can't."

"Okay." I suppose there's no sense arguing with her. "I could come there, and we could do something fun." I don't know why I can't leave well enough alone, but I just can't.

"Don't come," she tells me. "I really do have to start my job tomorrow and I have a lot to do here. Callie and her husband are staying with me until they can figure out their next step."

I'm not sure what her friend and her husband have to do with me coming out to lend my support, but Ashlyn's made it clear I'm not welcome. It's strange how much that hurts.

"Okay, then, well, I better get going," I tell her.

"To Maple Fest?" she wants to know.

"Maybe." My evasiveness is pure petulance but since Ashlyn has made it clear she doesn't want to see me, I don't feel the need to let her know what I'm up to.

"Have fun," she says, suddenly trying to sound like there's no tension between us.

"Will do." And then I hang up. No "Goodbye," no "Talk to you soon." I just hang up feeling butt hurt that Ashlyn means more to me than I mean to her.

THE FIRST PERSON I see when I walk into Maple Fest is Lucian Lowe. He's a defenseman for the Ice Breakers and honestly, one of the nicest guys I've ever met. If he were a dog, he'd be a golden retriever service dog. You know, sweet, playful, and above all else, helpful.

Lucian is with Neesha Gilmore. She runs a café inside a local bookshop, which I have yet to go into, but I understand it is first rate. She also has a cupcake business on the side. Neesha is the one whose cupcakes Ashlyn turned me on to when we went to the farmers' market together.

From what Lucian has told us, Neesha had a painful breakup with another hockey player, and she had vowed to never have anything to do with another one. That's why Lucian isn't telling her he's on the Ice Breakers. He's trying to win her over first. Which is the reason I don't go over to say hello. Lucian doesn't want Neesha to wonder why he has so many hockey player friends.

The next person I see is Dale. He's waiting in line at a stand selling apple cider donuts, and he's not alone. Walking up to him, I say, "I see you've found a friend, Coach."

Shirley May from the diner is by his side and she's wearing a smile that literally stretches from ear to ear. "Jamie," she says excitedly. "How are you doing? Where's Ashlyn?"

"She's gone back to LA," I tell her.

Shirley May's expression falters. "For good?"

I shove my hands in my pockets as my fingers clench into fists of frustration. "That's what she says."

Dale puts his arm around my shoulders consolingly. "That's too bad, son. I'm sorry."

"It's not like we were dating for real," I tell him. But it is Dale's fault we were even pretending to date and that is currently making me feel the tiniest bit hostile toward him.

Sensing my mood isn't good, he says, "She seemed like a nice girl."

"Nice?" Shirley May exclaims. "Ashlyn Thompkins is one of the best people I know. I was so hopeful that when she came home, she might stay." The diner owner's gaze shifts behind me. "Will you look at that. Mayor Thompkins has finally shown his face. We were all starting to think he was on his deathbed or something."

I turn around and see a hefty man of average height approach us. His arm is around a woman that I would know was

Ashlyn's mother anywhere. The two are lookalikes with the small exception of about thirty years.

The mayor and his wife approach us. "Dale," he calls out. "I hear your team is doing well."

As they close in, Dale shakes his hand. "Mayor. It's nice to see you again." Then he gestures toward Mrs. Thompkins. "This must be your lovely wife."

The mayor announces, "This is my beautiful Alicia." Ashlyn's mom smiles sweetly as she looks at her husband with borderline adoration. It appears Ashlyn knew what she was doing sending them away together.

Dale turns to me and says, "This is Jamie Hayes, our captain."

"Jamie!" The mayor seems inordinately pleased to meet me. "I'm sorry I missed our supper, but I understand Ashlyn took good care of you."

"Yes, sir," I tell him. "Your daughter was very kind to share a meal with me." I don't bother saying anything more because that would just be weird. Also, it's not like there's any reason to.

"What do you make of this business with Alexander MacDonald, Bill?" Shirley May asks the mayor.

"It's troubling, for sure," the mayor says. "But even so, I'm sure we'll figure this out together."

"We've missed seeing you around town," the diner owner tells him. "It's good to have you back on your feet."

"I left you in good hands," he says without confirming or denying the state of his health.

"Ashlyn would make a great mayor," Shirley May announces.

"From your mouth to God's ear, Shirley May. I've been telling her the same thing for a couple of years now, but I don't think she's getting the hint."

"Ashlyn has a big life in LA," Alicia Thompkins interjects. Then she tells her husband, "You got to choose your own path, now you let our daughter do the same."

The mayor looks at his wife lovingly. "Of course, dear. Anything you say."

After a moment of silence, I interject, "Well, I'm off to get a pretzel with that beer cheese sauce I've heard so much about. Good to see you all."

As I walk away, Dale calls out, "Remember what I told you when you first moved here."

I stop in my tracks before turning back to him. "Don't feed the bears?"

He laughs. "Well, obviously, but that's not what I'm talking about."

"Don't take candy from strangers?" I joke.

Another head shake. "Cupid lives in Maple Falls," he says with a wink.

Glancing in Shirley May's direction, I tell him, "Looks like that's working out for you."

His face illuminates like he just got hit with a spotlight. "I sure hope so, but I think it might work out for you, too."

I never told Dale that I was having feelings for Ashlyn, so I don't know what he's talking about. But then I turn to follow his gaze.

What in the world is Allegra still doing in town?

CHAPTER 35
ASHLYN

I'VE BEEN BACK in LA for two weeks and I can honestly say, it's felt strange the entire time. I first chalked this phenomenon up to the fact that I was worried my house was going to burn down, but the feeling didn't pass once the danger did. Instead, there's been a continued sense of unease.

According to my dad, things in Maple Falls have been wild. They found a loophole in some old document that makes it impossible for Alexander MacDonald to touch Main Street. Jeremy Hunt continues to create such a ruckus in town, I wouldn't be surprised if someone fitted him for cement boots and threw him in the river. And no one has seen Alexander MacDonald in person. All-in-all, everything is still so far up in the air that no one knows how this thing will play out.

Today is my first day working for my new client, famed talk show host, Estelle Rodrigues. Este, as she's commonly known, is nothing like I would expect her to be. As in, she's not the typical designer-hoarding clothes horse I usually work for. In fact, when she opened the door, she was wearing some woo woo caftan with outer space printed on it.

That's when I learned that Este hasn't engaged me to orga-nize her clothes closet at all. She's hired me to catalogue her massive collection of what she calls "alien artifacts and art." It was quite a shock to learn that she not only believes in beings from other worlds but that she's convinced they live here among us.

When she introduced me to my task this morning, she said, "I've always wondered how anyone could think that God's greatest creation was human. Doesn't it make you shudder to think we're the best the Divine could concoct?" She offers a shudder of her own. "We're just a bunch of war-mongering hate machines worshipping money. Does that sound like the God you know?"

I'd honestly never thought about it before, but after ruminating on it all afternoon, I think Este might be on to something.

I'm nearly done cataloguing her illustrations of some race she calls the Andromedins, when she walks into the room. "How are you doing?" she asks.

"Um, good," I tell her. "You have quite an interesting collection here."

"Thank you!" She takes my comment like it's a compliment. "I've been studying this field for decades now."

I'm really not sure what the proper response is so I keep it vague. "Oh."

"I have a message for you," Este tells me.

I stop what I'm doing and look at her. "Really? What?"

She puts her hands into her pants pockets before saying, "I don't think you're happy here."

"Excuse me?"

"Not here in my house, but in Los Angeles."

Is she psychic now, too? Before I can ask, she adds, "I don't think this is where you're meant to be."

"Why do you think that?" I ask nervously, my gaze shifting from side-to-side.

Her brown eyes twinkle as she says, "I've heard some things."

Before I can sensor myself, I blurt out, "From aliens?" I'm not trying to suggest aliens aren't real, but even if they are, I can't imagine I'm of any concern to them.

She laughs. "No, dear. I overheard you on the phone earlier talking about how things don't feel the same since you've come back from Washington."

I exhale loudly in relief. Este is an eavesdropper, not a channel for the other world. "It's been a strange reentry," I confess. Then for some reason, I tell her, "I met a guy when I was home. We didn't date or anything, but we became close."

"What's keeping you from finding out if there could be something more?" she asks.

I uncross my legs and push myself up from the floor, leaving a pile of illustrations behind. "I don't think I should have to change my life for a man," I tell her bluntly.

She nods her head knowingly. "I hear that. But there's all kinds of change, and not all of it is bad. Take me ..." She crosses the room and sits down on a loveseat by one of the many bookshelves. Motioning for me to join her, she says, "I must be thirty years older than you, and I was hellbent on proving myself in a man's world."

Sitting down next to her, I tell her, "You've done a heck of a job, too. Seriously, you're a legend."

She smiles, but only slightly. "While I appreciate that, and that's exactly what I set out to become, I didn't get everything I wanted in life."

"What didn't you get?"

"I never got married and I never had children. I would have loved both of those things very much."

"Why do think that never happened for you?" I feel like I'm intruding into her privacy, but she is the one who brought this up.

"Men have notoriously either felt threatened by me, or they've tried to get close to me in order to promote their own careers." Noticing the horrified expression on my face, she adds, "It's just been my path. But my point in bringing this up to you is to say that if there's something you want, you need to go for it."

"Even if it means changing my whole life?"

"Depends on what means more to you," she says. "Would you rather be a closet designer in LA or find a man you can build a life with?"

"You don't think I can have both?"

She shrugs her narrow shoulders. "Maybe. But here you are doing a job you love and all the while pining for a man who doesn't live here. Maybe you should go home and see what happens with him, and if things work out, you could come back to LA together."

"There's a bachelor auction tomorrow night ..." I start to say.

"Is your man up for sale?"

"He is. My hometown is trying to raise money to buy some acreage." I don't bother to explain the whole sordid story. "Jamie plays for our local NHL team, and his team has agreed to auction off the players to help raise money."

"You should go home and bid on him," she says.

I shake my head. "Bidding starts at five thousand dollars. I don't have that kind of spare cash." But even as I say that a thought pops into my head. Standing up, I walk across the room to where my purse is. I open it and pull out Zach Hart's business card.

Waving it in the air, I declare, "But I think I might know how to get it!"

As I am preparing to leave Este's house, she makes me promise that I'll stay in Maple Falls for at least a month. She feels this is the minimum amount of time to realistically see if Jamie and I might have a future together. "What about my job here?" I ask.

"I'll find someone else," she says before adding, "You're doing this for both of us, Ashlyn. I'm rooting for you."

When I get back to my house, I tell Callie about my plan. "You guys can stay here as long as you want," I tell her. "And if things work out and I wind up staying in Maple Falls for a while, you and Dillion can take over my lease."

Relief fills my friend's face. "That would be great. I don't think I'm prepared to buy here again. At least for now. In fact, I'm not sure I'm cut out for Southern California long-term."

"It's been a fun run though, huh?" I ask.

"Yes it has. But we've been talking about starting a family. I'd love to be able to take a few years off work to spend with my kids, and I know that isn't possible here."

"It's expensive, for sure."

Callie wraps her arms around me in a hug and announces, "I love you, Ash. Go find your happy ending."

I'm suddenly full of optimism that my life is working out exactly as it should. I can't wait to get home to Maple Falls and tell Jamie that.

CHAPTER 36
ASHLYN

MY PARENTS WERE THRILLED when I showed up on their doorstep unexpectedly last night. When I told them I plan to stay for at least a month, my dad asked if I could stay for two so he could leave me in charge of things while he and my mom spend the bulk of December in Italy. I promised to consider it.

I'm currently standing outside the Hawk River Lodge where the bachelor auction is going to take place. I'm wearing the same red dress I wore the night of the inaugural ball for the Ice Breakers.

The parking lot is packed, so I'm guessing we're going to make a ton of money tonight. My dad told me there are a bunch of wealthy single women who've flown in from all over the country to support our cause. I'm pretty sure *our cause* isn't their motivating factor. They're here to buy themselves a date with a professional hockey player, plain and simple.

I quickly check my coat before heading toward the back door of the ballroom. I didn't tell anyone I was going to be here, because I figure the element of surprise is a good thing. Also, I'm a little terrified.

My dad is talking to a couple of people, so I flag him to get his attention. He hurries toward me. "You look gorgeous, honey!" Then he recaps our plan. "I'll go out and remind everyone what we're doing here, and then I'll introduce you to get the ball rolling. How does that sound?"

My mouth is so dry I can only bob my head up and down in agreement.

As he walks away, I find a bottle of water and take slow sips. I'm a nervous wreck. It's been almost two weeks since I've talked to Jamie and I'm not even sure he'll be happy to see me. In fact, with my recent luck, he might already be dating someone else. The thought causes my stomach to tighten.

Making my way to stage right, I listen while my dad warms up the crowd. He thanks everyone for coming and assures them their contributions will help save Maple Falls. Then he expresses gratitude for their patience while he was "sick." Finally, he says, "I'd like to acknowledge my daughter, Ashlyn, for everything she did to help us while I was under the weather."

He reaches his arm out in my direction while adding, "She did such a great job that she's come home to see her wonderful idea through to the finish line." I walk out on stage to thundering applause.

When I reach my dad's side, I find my voice and tell him, "I may have started the ball rolling, but it's Maple Falls who deserves the applause tonight." Then I face the crowd and join them in praising our efforts.

When the celebration dies down, I step up to the podium. "What do you say we auction off some hockey players?" Hoots and whistles fill the air in support.

Looking down at the list in front of me, I don't see Jamie's name. Alarm fills me like a bad case of food poisoning. Why isn't he being auctioned off like he promised? I search the crowd in hopes of spotting him, but he's nowhere to be seen.

There's only one thing to do. I read the first name on the list and robotically start the proceedings. "Jackson Flint is our first player on the block! Will you please join me, Jackson?"

A tall and exceptionally handsome man stands up and makes

his way toward the stage. When he reaches my side, I ask the crowd, "Who would like to spend a couple of hours with Jackson?"

The room erupts again, and two women immediately jump to their feet and start waving their paddles in the air. "We're starting the bidding at five thousand dollars."

The blonde woman in the black leather corset shouts, "Eight thousand dollars!"

The other woman, who looks old enough to be her mother, calls out, "Ten!"

They go back and forth until the price tag reaches twenty-five thousand. The corset gets him.

The next several players go for varying amounts, but none of them come close to Jackson Flint. I take a short break when I notice a waitress has brought a glass of water for me. After assuring the crowd I'll be right back, I move off stage. Reaching for the glass, I tell her, "Thank you so much. I'm parched."

"This is fun, huh?" she responds. "I wish I had the money to get in on the action."

"What about that first guy?" I ask. "That was incredible."

She leans in close to me and whispers, "The two women bidding on him were his mother and sister."

Shocked, I ask, "How do you know that?"

"I heard them chatting in the ladies room. Jackson told them what to spend. According to the mom, his agent told him to make sure he went for a lot so they could try to negotiate more money for him next year."

"I don't think that's how it goes," I tell her.

She shrugs. "Who cares? We got another twenty-five grand in the kitty."

I feel a little relieved as I go back out on stage. But then I scan the audience and see Jamie. He's sitting with Allegra.

White hot jealousy with a chaser of fury hits me hard. Why is he here with her? Are they back together? I want answers and I want them now, but I have to keep on with the auction.

Looking at the next name on my list, I call out, "It's time for Clément Rivière to find a date! Clément, please join me."

The tall Frenchman stands up, looking extraordinarily uncomfortable. His gaze shifts around the room like he's considering running to the nearest exit. "This way, Clément," I encourage him while pointing to my side.

Once he's standing next to me, I tell the audience, "That's right, ladies—the accent is real, and so is his talent on the ice. On top of that, Clément Rivière is also restoring one of Maple Falls' most beloved properties to its former glory, the old MacDonald place."

"A man who can play goalie, bake soufflés, and is bringing back a bit of Maple Falls history. What more could you want? Shall we open the bidding?"

"Five thousand," Bernadette Huckle, the town's librarian, calls out. I suppress raw laughter at the thought that our mind-mannered town librarian is so eager to help out.

"Eight thousand!" another voice rings out.

"Eight thousand, one hundred!" The bids are slowing down a bit, but they keep coming.

"Eight thousand, two hundred!"

With every offer, Clément seems closer and closer to jumping out of his skin. When the price tag reaches nine thousand dollars, he leaves the stage and walks out into the audience. There, he grabs a paddle before rejoining me. "Nine thousand!" he shouts.

Covering the microphone, I tell him, "You don't bid for yourself."

"Nine thousand five hundred!" he yells.

"Clément, that's not how things are done. You need to let the audience bid."

"Why?" he demands. "I thought the whole point of this charade was to make money. My money is as good as theirs, no?" He waves his paddle at the crowd.

I suppose he's right. "Well folks, it appears we have an eccentric Frenchman on the team. Do we have any more offers?" I ask.

Everyone in the room appears to be in a state of shock at the odd turn of events but the bidding continues. We're well into the five-figures when it ends. "Okay then, I guess we can call it! The Frenchman wins a date with himself!"

Clément hands me his paddle and starts clapping for his win.

Looking down at my list, I see there's only one name left—Harry Franks. I glance out into the audience and make eye contact with Jamie. Without thinking things through, I announce, "Our next bachelor is the Ice Breakers' very own captain, Jamie Hayes!" I can't quite read his expression, but I'd say it's somewhere between shock and horror.

Jamie stands up slowly before joining me on stage. When he arrives, he whispers, "What are you doing?"

Reaching out, I click off the microphone before telling him, "You promised to be auctioned off if I agreed to be your fake girlfriend. I did my part."

"You left town," he hisses.

"I thought my house was going to burn down!" I yell at him. Who needs a microphone when there's irritation?

"But you didn't come back."

"I had to work," I tell him with less heat.

"You stopped calling," he accuses.

"You didn't call me either," I retort.

"That's because you made it perfectly clear you wanted nothing to do with me."

"So, you went back to your ex-girlfriend?" I'm back to shouting. But instead of letting him answer, I turn the microphone back on. The high-pitched squeal that results is enough to cause hearing loss.

"Jamie Hayes, folks! Who wants to bid five thousand?"

I see a couple of paddles go up, so I raise the amount. "Ten thousand!"

One paddle this time. It's Allegra. I'm so mad I could spit

bullets. "Thirty thousand!" I don't even bother to see if Allegra's still a contender. Instead, I grab the paddle Clément left behind and call out, "Thirty thousand! Going once, twice, gone! I win the date with Jamie Hayes!"

Jamie looks so startled you could probably blow him over with a slight breeze. "Where in the world did you get thirty thousand dollars?" he wants to know.

"You can ask me that on our date," I tell him before pushing him off stage.

My head is spinning so much I don't even remember auctioning off Harry Franks. All I know is that in the end we made a huge dent in the amount of money we're going to offer to Alexander MacDonald. Thirty thousand of which was graciously donated by Zach Hart so I could win a date with Jamie.

A date I'm quite honestly terrified to go on.

CHAPTER 37
JAMIE

I COULD NOT BELIEVE my eyes when I saw that Ashlyn came back for the bachelor auction. Particularly when she called my name after I dropped out. I wasn't planning to stiff the town, either. I was just going to donate to them directly.

I didn't get a chance to talk to Ashlyn when the auction ended because she hightailed it out of there like her dress was on fire. Her gorgeous, red, slinky dress that made me want to put my coat on her so no one else could enjoy the view.

I'm currently on my way to Shirley May's, where she requested we meet for our date. As I walk into the restaurant, I realize that no one else is here, which is weird because Shirley May's is a staple in this town and always busy.

But then I see Ashlyn. She's sitting at the same booth where we had dinner together the night she came in her dad's place. Even though she's not wearing the red dress, she's easily the most beautiful woman I've ever seen.

I approach slowly, all the while keeping my gaze glued to hers. When I stop next to her, she says, "Jamie. Thank you for coming."

"You did buy me," I remind her.

"I did." She gestures for me to sit down.

Sliding into the booth across from her, I ask, "What are you doing here?"

"Aren't we on a date?" She looks confused.

"What are you doing back in Maple Falls? I thought you didn't plan on returning."

"I didn't, but I changed my mind."

"Why?" I want to know.

She lowers her eyes until she's looking at the table. "I forgot something,"

"Your clothes?" I ask.

She shakes her head.

"Your toothbrush?"

Her eyes suddenly meet mine. "I forgot that I was starting to believe in fate."

I quirk an eyebrow in response, so she continues, "I got to thinking that a lot of events had to occur for you and me to find ourselves in Maple Falls at the same time."

She doesn't give me a chance to respond. Instead, she says, "Allegra isn't the woman for you, Jamie."

While I know this, I still feel the need to ask, "Why do you say that?"

"Because I am. I think I'm the woman for you."

Well, what do you know? I did not see this coming, but I want to hear it from her. "Is that so?"

"I know you were with her at the lodge, and you didn't let yourself be auctioned off because you're back with her, but it's the wrong decision, Jamie. She's hurt you before, and she'll do it again."

I sit silently for a moment before announcing, "Allegra and I are not back together."

Ashlyn looks disbelieving. "What do you mean you're not back together? I saw you at the auction with her."

I take a sip from the water glass in front of me before telling her, "We weren't together."

"She was sitting right next to you," Ashlyn says accusingly.

"That's because she's been in town since the day after you left. She's been stalking me in order to get me to change my mind about going back to New York with her. She was waiting for me when I showed up at the auction and she followed me in."

Ashlyn doesn't seem to know what to believe, so I tell her, "My heart hasn't been on the market since the night I met you."

Her upper lip quivers with emotion. "That wasn't a date."

"Maybe not, but I knew deep down my life would never be the same."

"Because of me?" She blinks her green eyes, setting loose a single tear.

"Because of you, Ashlyn. I never wanted you to leave Maple Falls, and when you did, I wanted to go with you. There hasn't been a minute where you haven't been on my mind."

Reaching her hands across the table, she gently touches my forearms. "Are you serious? You want to date me? Even after you told me you weren't interested in dating anyone?"

"I want to date you, Ashlyn. I want to date you very much."

Shirley May pops her head out from around the back corner. I hear the loud popping sound before I see the bottle of champagne in her hands. "I told you she was coming home!" Then she hurries toward us and pours our drinks.

I turn to Ashlyn and ask, "*Are* you coming home?"

"For now," she says. "If things work out for us though, maybe you'll consider moving to LA with me at some point."

I clink my glass against hers, and tell her, "I'm pretty sure I'd move to the moon with you, Ashlyn."

And just like that, fate has changed my life, and I couldn't be more grateful.

EPILOGUE—ASHLYN

THIS YEAR, Thanksgiving has brought more gratitude than ever before. Jamie and I are officially a couple and our relationship is more amazing than I could have ever dreamed. Even though I spend a lot of time at Town Hall with my dad, I haven't gotten a real job yet, so I'm able to go to all of Jamie's games. Even the away ones. As such, our connection has become so strong I can no longer imagine what my life would look like without him.

As expected, the bears went into hibernation in late October and freed Jamie to move back to his cabin. He's decided not to rush into buying something now that he has a few months of peace in front of him.

My parents' marriage is better than it's ever been. My dad has lightened up on his obsession with Maple Falls and has even talked about leaving his term early. Phillip couldn't be happier—the big doody.

The big news is that Maple Falls has been saved! It was super touch and go with Alexander MacDonald and the town, but things took a turn when a note from Victor MacDonald was found in a time capsule. In it, he conveyed his love for Maple Falls and his hope that his ancestors would live here for generations to come. That was enough for old Alexander not only to give up his rights to any land, but he now wants to spend part of his year living here.

The truth is that Alexander MacDonald is nothing like his representative, Jeremy, had us believe. He's a lovely man who had no idea what was being said and done in his name. He's assured my dad that he is personally going to make sure that Maple Falls stays just the way his ancestor wanted it to.

We are now going to use all the money we had raised to buy the land to help our town in various ways. Things have turned out better than we could have hoped. It's almost like this was our fate.

I hurried to send out a few texts spreading the good news before sitting down to Thanksgiving supper with my mom, dad, Jamie, Dale Hauser, and Shirley May.

The turkey is huge, and the table is brimming with all the fixings. The flickering candles create dancing shadows that move across the room making everything feel like a really amazing dream.

As is our tradition, my dad stands up first and raises his wine glass. "Gratitude is the key component of happiness," he says. "And this year, I am full of gratitude." He turns to my mom, "Alicia, you are the love of my life. You have stood beside me and held me up in times of trouble; you have given me a family; you have made a home for us that has offered incomparable comfort. You are my heart and my life. I would be nothing without you, and I vow to spend every day that I have left on this earth showing you how grateful I am for you."

A slow smile crosses my mother's face as she raises her glass to him and says, "I'd like to have that comment notarized, please." Everyone laughs. Then she continues, "I am also grateful for you, Bill, but I'm most thankful for our beautiful daughter Ashlyn." She turns her glass to me. "Honey, you are the most kindhearted person I know. You are strong and courageous. You are caring and thoughtful. Had you not come home to help your father and me, this would have been a very different Thanksgiving. And not for the better." Leaning over, she taps her glass to mine. "To you, my darling. You have all my thanks."

Dale and Shirley May both offer their gratitude for the year, as well. I don't listen to them closely because my eyes are glued to Jamie. When it's his turn, he stands up and directs his toast to Dale. "I know you're all expecting me to say I'm most thankful for Ashlyn. And while I truly am awed to have such an amazing woman in my life"—he winks in my direction—" I would not be here had my old friend Dale Hauser not called and asked me to join his new team. Dale," Jamie says, "you have always had my back, and I want you to know that I will always have yours."

When it's finally my turn, I stand up and move my glass around from person to person. "I'm thankful to you all. This year has been full of lessons and full of blessings, and I couldn't have gotten through it without every one of you." With mischievous intent, I turn toward Shirley May. "But my dear friend Shirley May has brought the pecan praline pie, and for that, I am the most grateful!"

The table fills with laughter, and as I sit down, I realize I truly am the most fortunate person I know. I thought my life was going one direction, and I resisted change because I couldn't see anything else for myself. Yet, nothing is set in stone. Sometimes, the harder things are, the bigger the reward for getting through them. The last couple of months have taught me that in spades.

Jamie reaches under the table and takes my hand in his. Then he leans over and whispers, "I'm so grateful for you, Ashlyn. Being with you feels like home."

I squeeze his hand. "Home isn't a place," I tell him. "Home is where your people are."

I've only been back in Maple Falls for a month. But I'm committed to staying for much longer should that be my fate. I vow to keep my heart open to whatever life's journey has in store for me, and to the best of my ability, I'll try to ride the ride with courage and gratitude.

WELCOME BACK TO MAPLE FALLS—THE small town where hockey players fall in love! This is a multi-author series of seven full-length books that could be read as standalones, but we think you'll enjoy them best in order.

Breaking the Ice by Whitney Dineen

Offside and Off-Limits by Kate O'Keeffe

Checking Mr. Wrong by Anne Kemp

Skating & Faking Dating by Ellie Hall

Goalie and the Girl Next Door by Elsie Woods

Soulmates and Slapshots by Melissa Baldwin

The Icing on the Cake by Grace Worthington

If you missed the first series, Love on Thin Ice, and want to know how it all began, check out the first seven books by the same group of authors. Please note, they all stand alone, but reading them together will provide a richer and cozier small town hockey romance reading experience.

Breaking the Ice by Whitney Dineen

The Rebound Play by Kate O'Keeffe

The Friend Face-Off by Grace Worthington

Love in Overtime by Melissa Baldwin

The Parent Playbook by Elsie Woods

Love at First Skate by Ellie Hall

Penalties and Proposals by Anne Kemp

GRAB THE NEXT BOOK IN THE SERIES, WHERE CLARA AND CADE GET THEIR CHANCE, IN:

OFFSIDE AND OFF-LIMITS BY KATE O'KEEFFE

I survived chronic illness and a cheating ex. Surely I can resist one charming hockey player...right?

Clara

Working as the social media manager for a pro hockey team is all fun and games—until you trip into the arms of their biggest flirt during a livestream. Now the fans are shipping us, my boss is thrilled with the engagement, and I'm stuck dodging feelings for Cade Lennox, aka the certified charmer. The problem? My contract says he's off-limits. My heart, unfortunately, didn't get the memo.

Cade

I came to this small town to turn over a new leaf. But you know what they say about the best laid plans. All bets are off the second Clara Johnson literally stumbles into my arms and straight into my heart. She's focused, loyal, and the most beautiful challenge I've ever met. All I have to do is prove I'm worth the risk.

Offside and Off-Limits is part of the *Love in Maple Falls* sweet hockey romcom multi-author series. It's a forbidden love story between one flirty hockey player and the team's social media manager in this small town romance with all the sizzle and chemistry, but none of the spice.

CAST OF CHARACTERS IN MAPLE FALLS

Asher Tremblay: love interest is Mabel McCluskey; Position: Defense, #5. From Canada, played for the River City Renegades before being called up to the Ice Breakers.

Ashlyn Thompkins: love interest is Jamie Hayes; Grew up in Maple Falls across the street from Mabel McCluskey and next door to Clara and Keira Johnson; Mayor's daughter.

Bailey Porter: love interest is Carson Crane; Maple Falls local and friends with Mabel, Neesha, and Clara Johnson. Works for the NHL. Maple butter maker.

Cade Lennox: love interest is Clara Johnson; Position: Right wing, #44; played on the New York City Blades with Jamie Hayes.

Carson Crane: love interest is Bailey Porter; Position: Left wingman, #49. From Alabama, played for the Nebraska Knights, and was a last-minute transfer..

interest is Cade Lennox; sister of Keira
Maple Falls across the street from Mabel
next door to Ashlyn Thompkins; friends with
sufferer: Ice Breakers social media manager

re: love interest is Marcy Fontaine. Position:
Goa.   cently moved to the U.S.A. from France, where he
played for u..e Paris Lions, to follow his American Dream.

Fiona Hale: love interest is Weston Smith. From New York City,
visiting her aunt Denise Hale in Maple Falls.

Jamie Hayes: love interest is Ashlyn Thompkins; Position:
Center, #33; played on the New York City Blades with Cade
Lennox.

Lucian Lowe: love interest is Neesha Gilmore; Position:
Defenseman, #7. Played on the Carolina Crushers with Dawson
Hayes (series 1).

Mabel McCluskey: love interest is Asher Tremblay; daughter of
town gossip Mary-Ellen McCluskey, high school friends with
Neesha. Knows Fiona through work connections in NYC; grew
up in Maple Falls across the street from Clara and Keira Johnson.

Marcy Fontaine: love interest is Clément Rivière; works at
Happy Horizons ranch in exchange for room and board; Is an
accountant and most of the folks and Town Hall in Maple Falls.

Neesha Gilmore: love interest is Lucian Lowe; a cupcake baker
who lives in Maple Falls; works at the Falling for Books Cafe
with Emmy Roberts (series 1).

Weston Smith: love interest is Fiona Hale; Position: Defense,

#22. Former player with the Tennessee Wolves; knows Cooper Montgomery.

ABOUT THE AUTHOR

USA Today Bestseller Whitney Dineen is a rock star in her own head. While delusional about her singing abilities, there's been a plethora of validation that she's a fairly decent author (AMAZING!!!).

After winning many writing awards and selling nearly a kabillion books (math may not be her forte, either), she's decided to let the voices in her head say whatever they want (sorry, Mom). She also won a fourth-place ribbon in a fifth-grade swim meet in backstroke. So, there's that.

Whitney loves to play with her kids (a.k.a. dazzle them with her amazing flossing abilities), bake stuff, eat stuff, and write books for people who "get" her. She thinks french fries are the perfect food and Mrs. Roper is her spirit animal.

Join her newsletter for news of her latest releases, sales, and recommendations. If you consider yourself a superfan, join her private reader group, where you will be offered the chance to read her books before they're released.

ALSO BY WHITNEY DINEEN

Pity Series

Pity Date

Pity Party

Pity Pact

Pity Parade

Pity Present

Pity Play

Pity Please (Coming Soon)

The Mimi Chronicles

The Reinvention of Mimi Finnegan

Mimi Plus Two

Kindred Spirits

Relatively Series

Relatively Normal

Relatively Sane

Relatively Happy

Creek Water Series

The Event

The Move

The Plan

The Dream

Seven Brides for Seven Mothers Series

Love is a Battlefield

Ain't She Sweet

It's My Party

You're So Vain

Head Over Feet

Queen of Hearts

At Last

She Sins at Midnight

Going Up?

Love for Sale

The Accidentally in Love Series (with Melanie Summers)

Text Me on Tuesday

The Text God

Text Wars

Text in Show

Mistle Text

Text and Confused

A Gamble on Love Mom-Com Series (with Melanie Summers)

No Ordinary Hate

A Hate Like This

Hate, Rinse, Repeat

Love on Thin Ice/Love in Maple Falls

Breaking the Ice

Fake-Off with Fate

Conspiracy Thriller

See No More

Non-Fiction Humor

Motherhood, Martyrdom & Costco Runs

Middle Reader

Wilhelmina and the Willamette Wig Factory

Who the Heck is Harvey Stingle?

Children's Books

The Friendship Bench